'I don't want you here. My health is not your concern.'

Tiggy folded her arms. 'That's tough. I'm not going anywhere. Nick, why didn't you tell me you'd been badly injured? You were in Intensive Care and you didn't even let me know!'

But was she really surprised? Two years after they were married Nick had stopped talking to her about the important things.

'What difference would it have made? Our marriage was—is—over.'

'I'm not likely to forget that,' she retorted. 'Look, Nick, I'm here now. Can't we at least be civil to each other?'

He glared at her but she refused to look away. Suddenly the grim line of his mouth softened, and when he smiled she caught a glimpse of the Nick she had first known. Her insides melted.

'Sorry. Of course.' He dragged a hand across the stubble on his cheek. 'Forgive me.'

As he turned away to take something from his locker she studied him more carefully. He might have changed, but he still made her catch her breath. She still remembered the feel of him, remembered every inch of his body—the hard muscles of his abdomen, his long legs and powerful thighs, the feel of his fingertips on her skin, the planes of his face under hers. She bit back a groan and closed her eyes.

Six years and he still made her pulse race. Six years since she'd seen him and one glance was enough for her to know she'd never got him out of her head. She should get the hell away from him—simply walk out through the door. Not just walk, run—as fast as her legs could carry her.

Dear Reader

I have long been fascinated with the role men and women (particularly women) have played in war, wondering how I would have coped with the fear and horror.

A couple of years ago I heard a doctor speaking about his time in Iraq, when he accompanied soldiers on patrol, and found his talk riveting. A few months later I watched a documentary series about the men and women who care for the wounded at Camp Bastion, the main British military base in Afghanistan. One episode in particular, in which a nurse had to accompany the doctor into a firing zone in order to rescue a badly injured man, had me thinking. What kind of men and women would risk their lives in order to save the life of another?

So when my editor asked me if I wanted to write the first book in a military duo with a fellow author, the wonderful Tina Beckett, I leaped at the chance and *Men of Honour* was born.

Dr Nick Casey is an army doctor who feels responsible for the men and women under his care. Tiggy is a nurse in Afghanistan for a short tour. When they first meet, sparks fly.

But when Nick can't stay away from Afghanistan, it seems their love isn't enough to keep them together.

I hope I have successfully conveyed the reality of a medic's life in a war situation while keeping Nick and Tiggy's love story at the forefront.

I would love to know what you think. You can find me on Facebook at www.facebook.com/AnneFraserAuthor or on my blog at http://annefraserauthor.wordpress.com

Best wishes

Anne

Book Two in the *Men of Honour* duet
THE LONE WOLF'S CRAVING by Tina Beckett
is also available this month
from Mills & Boon® Medical Romance™

THE WIFE HE
NEVER FORGOT

BY
ANNE FRASER

First published in Great Britain 2013
by Mills & Boon, an imprint of Harlequin (UK) Limited.
Harlequin (UK) Limited, Eton House, 18-24 Paradise Road,
Richmond, Surrey TW9 1SR

© Anne Fraser 2013

ISBN: 978 0 263 23375 9

Harlequin (UK) policy is to use papers that are natural, renewable and recyclable products and made from wood grown in sustainable forests. The logging and manufacturing process conform to the legal environmental regulations of the country of origin.

Printed and bound in Great Britain
by CPI Antony Rowe, Chippenham, Wiltshire

Anne Fraser was born in Scotland, but brought up in South Africa. After she left school she returned to the birthplace of her parents, the remote Western Islands of Scotland. She left there to train as a nurse, before going on to university to study English Literature. After the birth of her first child she and her doctor husband travelled the world, working in rural Africa, Australia and Northern Canada. Anne still works in the health sector. To relax, she enjoys spending time with her family, reading, walking and travelling.

Recent titles by Anne Fraser:

These books are also available in eBook format from www.millsandboon.co.uk

To my wonderful, encouraging and patient editor,
Megan Haslam.

PROLOGUE

NICK HAD BEEN leaning against the wall of their temporary shelter, checking his rifle and thinking of nothing much, when all hell broke loose.

As the part of the troop that had remained behind exploded into action, he retrieved his Kevlar helmet and peered over the wall of the sangar.

'Keep your head down, sir!' one of the men shouted as he rushed past and took up his firing position immediately in front of Nick.

Nick did as he suggested, just as a bullet whizzed over the top of his head and landed in the wall behind him in an explosion of dust.

It was supposed to be a routine patrol where his platoon would join up with the Americans to decide how far north they should go before setting up a base.

'Man down!' The anguished cry came over the radio.

Nick glanced around. They'd arrived thirty minutes ago and there had only been time to set up a small receiving space in the overhang of the rock that they were using as the temporary forward operating base.

Adrenaline tore through him. This was what he'd trained for. He had to ignore what was going on below and concentrate on any casualties.

But damn, if he needed a medevac for any of them, it

was going to be difficult. He would worry about that later. Right now he had to focus on the present.

The first casualty to be brought back to the relative safety of the sangar was the medic. Luckily, he had no more than a bullet graze to his arm and someone had already applied a temporary dressing.

'I need to get back out there, sir,' he yelled. 'It's only a graze.'

'It might be only a graze but it's going to keep you out of action for a few days,' Nick responded firmly.

Quickly he examined the wound. The bullet had passed through the flesh of the medic's upper arm. Right now there was little Nick could do except clean it again and rebandage it. When they got him back to camp he would do a more thorough job. Perhaps, with a bit of luck, they'd get out of this with only this one casualty.

But it wasn't to be. The sound of gunfire increased, as did the noise on the radio.

'Five men pinned down—Americans among them,' Captain Forsythe muttered. 'They're holing up in one of the empty houses. My men can't get to them.'

'Injuries?' Nick asked.

The captain nodded. 'At least one down. That's all I know.'

Nick risked another glance over the wall. Beneath him, about fifty metres away, was the deserted village the soldiers had been searching.

Nick picked up his bag and headed for the wall.

'Where the hell do you think you're going?' Captain Forsythe snapped.

Nick barely glanced at him. 'There's a man out there. If he's not dead, he's badly injured. I'm a doctor—and a soldier. Where the hell do you think I'm going?'

* * *

Nick, accompanied by several of the soldiers, zigzagged his way towards the house and the wounded soldier.

He had his own rifle slung over his shoulder. As part of the platoon he was obliged to carry a weapon but was only required to use it in self-defence. Whether he would was not a question he chose to ask himself.

As bullets spat into the ground he concentrated on one thing and one thing only: getting to the injured man, hopefully in one piece.

He leapt over a low wall and into the deserted house, conscious of two of the men from his own company following close behind him while the remainder of the soldiers continued to lay down covering fire.

The casualty was an American. Not that it mattered. His job was to treat the injured regardless of nationality, and that included the enemy.

The soldier was conscious but bleeding from a nasty wound to his shoulder. As Nick set about putting up a drip he asked one of the soldiers to call for a medevac.

'You'll be lucky, sir,' Private Johnston muttered. 'Don't know how the 'copter can land with all this going on.'

'Just let them know we're going to need them whenever they can make it, Private, ' Nick said. 'Hold onto the drip for me while I dress his wound.'

A shadow fell across the door as another American appeared at the doorway.

'Have you got Brad?' he demanded. 'Is he all right?'

'For God's sake, get down!' Nick yelled. Was the American crazy?

Just then there was an explosion that robbed Nick of his breath. He was flung backwards as debris rained through the narrow doorway.

It took him a few moments to catch his breath. He was

lying on his back with something heavy on top of him. He spat dust from his mouth.

'Johnston!'

'Over here, sir. I'm all right.'

'Our patient?'

'He's okay too. But don't think I can say the same about the other one.'

Nick became aware that the weight pinning him down was the young American who only seconds before had been standing at the door. His body had probably shielded him and the others.

'Help me here, Johnston.' Gently he rolled the soldier from on top of him, feeling the sticky wetness of blood. Poor sod hadn't stood a chance.

But as he sat up he became aware that the soldier was conscious.

'My leg,' he groaned.

Smoke clouded their small shelter and Nick used a torch to examine the young American. Blood was spurting from his groin, soaking into the dirt floor.

'What's your name, soldier?' he asked.

'Luke.'

'Okay, Luke. Stay still while I have a look at your leg.'

But the blood pumping from Luke's groin told Nick everything he needed to know. Shrapnel had pierced his femoral artery and the boy—because that was all he was—was bleeding to death in front of him. His pulse was thready and his skin had taken on the damp sheen of shock.

'Is it bad?' the wounded soldier asked.

The lad needed to be in hospital. He probably had twenty minutes at the most.

Not long enough, then.

Damn it.

Another explosion rent the air and it sounded as if the gunfire was getting closer.

'We need to get the hell out of here,' Johnston said.

Nick jammed his fist into the hole in the young soldier's leg. 'He can't be moved.'

'Go!' Luke's voice was faint. 'You gotta leave me. I'm not going to make it.' Every word was coming with increasing difficulty.

He would almost certainly bleed to death before they got him back to the sangar and Nick couldn't leave him here on his own—even if he knew there was almost no chance of saving his life. Nick made up his mind.

'Johnston, get two men to take the other man back to the sangar. Tell them to let Captain Forsythe know I need the medevac. Now!'

'I'll stay with you.'

'No. Get the hell out of here. This man and I will be fine.'

'But, sir!'

Nick cursed. 'That's an order, Johnston.'

The soldier hesitated. 'I'll be back for you as soon as I can.'

As Nick turned his attention again to the wounded American he was only dimly aware of Johnston and another soldier taking Brad, the other casualty, from the room.

'Get out of here,' Luke murmured. 'Save yourself. I don't want someone to die because of me.'

'I'm not going anywhere, son.' Nick cut the soldier's combat trousers away, struggling to see the wound for the blood. He did the same with his jacket and shirt. He needed to make sure Luke wasn't bleeding anywhere else. *Look beyond the obvious* was the mantra for an A and E surgeon. It was the ignored and uninvestigated that often killed.

As he worked he noted that Luke had an eagle tattooed on his right biceps. That wasn't unusual—for a soldier *not* to have a tattoo would have been noteworthy—but the soldier also had a scar that ran diagonally across his chest. This was no aftermath of surgery.

However, Nick had no time to wonder about past wounds. He inserted the venflon into a vein and, mercifully, Luke lost consciousness. Now he could get fluids into him, but he had to stop the bleeding. It was the only way to save the boy's life. Pressure wouldn't be enough. He would have to find the artery and clamp it—a procedure that was tricky enough in the luxury of a fully equipped theatre and with the help of experienced staff. But here? Almost no chance.

Nevertheless, he had to try. Even if he managed to stop him from bleeding to death, it was likely that Luke would lose his leg. But better a limb than his life.

The impact of the shrapnel had blown part of Luke's trousers into the wound, obscuring Nick's view even further. He took the clamp from his bag and took a deep breath as he tried to find the bleeder. It was almost impossible in the dim light of the house, without the blood and pieces of uniform further obscuring his view.

Working more by instinct than anything else, Nick clamped down on what he hoped was the right place. To his relief, almost immediately the blood stopped pumping from the wound.

Nick sat back on his haunches and wiped the sweat from his eyes with the back of his sleeve.

He'd stopped the bleeding, but if there was to be a hope in hell of saving Luke's life, he needed to get him back to the hospital at the camp.

He became aware that the gunfire was more sporadic

now and in the distance he could hear the powerful blades of a Chinook.

There was still a chance.

CHAPTER ONE

A year later

IT WAS HOT. Forty degrees Celsius and it was only just after six in the morning. The dust was everywhere, swirling around like dirty talcum powder coating the inside of her mouth and settling on every inch of her exposed skin.

Tiggy swigged from the water in her bottle, which was already turning tepid in the heat, brushed a damp curl from her forehead and sighed. The shower she'd had ten minutes before had been a complete waste of time.

She bent her head against a sudden dust ball. Everything was the same dun colour: the tents; her uniform; the Jeeps—there were even dust-coloured tanks parked along the high walls surrounding the compound. Tiggy didn't know if that made her feel better or worse.

She must have been crazy to come. Although back in the UK they had been thoroughly briefed as to what to expect—down to practising what medical emergencies they might encounter in a mock-up of a building with soldiers acting the part of casualties—nothing had really prepared her for the reality of living in a war zone. And nothing had prepared her for the sheer terror she felt.

Coming in to land last night on the Hercules, the pilot had dimmed the cabin lights in case they attracted enemy fire. When his words had come over the intercom, Tiggy had almost lost it.

Enemy fire? She hadn't signed up for that. She'd signed up to be looking after soldiers miles away from danger in a camp protected by soldiers.

She'd squeezed her eyes shut, not even able to force them open when she'd felt someone sit next to her. She had become aware of a faint scent of citrus.

'You can open your eyes, you know.' The laughter in his voice bugged her.

She'd opened one eye and squinted. In the dim light of the cabin all she had been able to make out had been a powerful frame in uniform and the flash of even, white teeth.

Whoever it was had been studying her frankly in return.

'For all you know, I'm having a nap,' she'd said through clenched teeth.

'I've never seen anyone nap while holding on to their seat so tight their knuckles were white.'

'God!' She gave up all pretence. 'What if they hit the plane? I'm scared to death of flying as it is.'

'Hey, relax. It will be okay. The pilots have done it scores of times and no one has shot them down yet. They just say what they do to make all the newbies cra— Apologies, ma'am. To scare the newbies.'

She hadn't been sure she'd entirely believed him, but she had felt a little better.

'How much longer until we're on the ground?'

'Another twenty minutes or so.'

'Twenty bloody minutes!' she groaned.

'Why don't you tell me all about yourself? It'll help distract you.' He held out a hand. 'I'm Nick, one of the army doctors. You?'

'Tiggy. Casualty nurse.'

'Then we'll be working together,' he said with a sideways grin. 'You with anyone? Married? Engaged?'

This was not exactly the sort of route Tiggy wanted to go down. Men didn't exactly queue up at her door. Might have been something to do with the fact that her brothers appeared to think it was their duty to guard her honour as if she were some early-twentieth-century maiden, or it might—and this was more likely—have to do with the fact that she wasn't particularly pretty or vivacious.

'No. You?'

'God, no!' He laughed.

The sound of sniggering came from the seats behind them.

'Major Casey married?' A soldier leant over the top of her seat. 'You have got to be kidding. The major barely stays with a woman long enough to—'

'That's enough, Corporal.' The words were quietly spoken but stopped the soldier from finishing his sentence.

Stay with a woman long enough to what?

The plane lurched to the right and Tiggy yelped.

'You have a strong grip for such a little thing,' Nick drawled.

She hadn't realised that she'd grabbed his hand, but when she tried to pull away he curled his fingers around hers.

It was easier to leave her hand where it was. Especially when it felt so reassuring—or would have if it weren't for the millions of little sparks, enough to ignite the whole plane, shooting up the side of her arm.

Adrenaline made you over-sensitive, didn't it?

'So, tell me, what made you come out here?' Nick asked.

Anyone would have thought they were on a day trip to the seaside.

'Brothers. One in Engineers, the other an Apache pilot. Thought I'd better come and check up on them.'

'I'm surprised they let you come out.'

'Let me? You mean you think I should have asked their permission?' Actually, if they had known she was planning to head out after them to a war zone, she had no doubt they would have stopped her—forcibly if necessary.

They might all be adults now, but her two brothers continued to protect their little sister as they had all their lives. Although they liked to spoil her, there were disadvantages to having older brothers.

'If I had a sister I wouldn't let her come out here,' Nick continued. 'No way. Women have no place in a war.'

Even if that was almost exactly what her family thought, Tiggy wasn't prepared to let it pass. 'Oh, for goodness' sake! This is the twenty-first century.'

'Doesn't matter. Women should be safe.'

'Barefoot, pregnant and in the kitchen? Please!' She had only just got started on putting him right when the plane lurched once more. She yelped again.

The I-told-you-so look he gave her was enough to make her decide that even if the plane went into a spiral she'd rather die than let him hear her scream.

Die? God, don't let her mind go there.

She took a deep breath. 'Just because I'm a little frightened of flying, it doesn't mean I shouldn't have come here.' She lifted her chin and stared at him. 'I'll be fine once we're on the ground.' At least her voice sounded reasonably steady.

He laughed. 'Good on you. Now, why don't you tell me about those brothers of yours?'

When the plane touched down with a skipping bounce, Tiggy was surprised. Despite her terror, the last twenty minutes or so had flown past. She realised that she'd told

Nick about her brothers, her parents, every place her father had been posted and even the family's pet dog, Hannibal.

God, she'd been babbling so much Nick knew almost everything about her life. On the other hand, she knew nothing about him. Probably because she hadn't let him get a word in edgeways.

Her companion returned her hand—she hadn't even realised she was still holding onto it—and eased out of his seat.

He touched his cap in a mock salute. 'See you around, Lieutenant.'

Tired and disoriented, Tiggy had only a vague recollection of being shown to her quarters by a friendly nurse in army uniform who had greeted her sleepily, shown her to her bunk and then, with a yawn, excused herself with a 'Catch you at breakfast'.

Even if the bed had been comfortable, Tiggy doubted she would have slept anyway. The adrenaline that was still making her heart hammer would have kept her awake even if she'd had a feather mattress to sleep on. And as for the heat! She couldn't remember being as hot during the day as she had been last night. Plus she was sure her foot had been chomped to bits by some horrible insect through the night.

How the hell was she going to manage six weeks of this? She'd have to. She doubted if the British Army would put on a special plane to fly her back out.

She straightened the collar of her uniform and took a deep breath. *Courage, girl*, she told herself. *You can do this.*

The mess tent was a hive of activity and noise as soldiers and medics helped themselves to breakfast. Tiggy looked around, unsure of what the correct protocol was. She didn't want to make more of an idiot of herself than she'd done on the flight. She tried to swallow past the lump in her throat. She had never felt so lonely, or so out of her depth.

A familiar smell drifted on the air. Coffee! That would make it better. She'd never be able to force solid food down her constricted throat but she'd kill for a cup of coffee. Wrong choice of words. She felt the tension in her limbs ease as a bubble of nervous laughter rose to the surface.

Someone came from behind and touched her on the elbow, and Tiggy jumped.

'You look lost.' It was Sue, the nurse from last night who'd showed her to her accommodation. Sue lowered her voice 'And absolutely terrified. Don't worry, we all felt the same way when we first arrived. In a day or two everything will seem as familiar as the good old NHS.'

Tiggy managed a smile. 'I doubt that.'

'You'll see, I'm never wrong.' Sue pressed a mug of coffee into her hands. 'Get that down you. You'll feel better. If you want breakfast, help yourself from over there.' She nodded in the direction of a counter where cheerful men in army fatigues were piling plates high with what looked like a full English breakfast. 'But I'd stay away from the scrambled eggs. They're powdered. Yuck.'

Tiggy shook her head. 'I think I'll give breakfast a miss, thanks all the same.'

Sue smiled. 'Can't say I blame you. But you'll get used to the food in the same way you'll get used to everything else. Finish your coffee and I'll take you across to the hospital and show you around. We've fifteen minutes before rounds.'

Tiggy took a grateful swig of coffee and almost spat it out. It was the worst she had ever tasted. And if Sue thought the eggs were bad... She gave herself a mental shake. Where was her usual optimism? Okay, the food might be rubbish, but she was always meaning to go on a diet—so what better way to give it a kick start? And if the coffee was hot, she would get used to that too.

Her mood improved further when she saw the hospital. Divided into separate sections, it had two well-equipped theatres, a resus area as well as a couple of wards and three intensive-care beds.

Looking at the facilities, she felt reassured. She could almost forget she was in the desert on the edge of a war zone—until the low rumble of an explosion made the building shudder. When no one else even flinched, she forced herself to concentrate on what Sue was saying

'You'll have been briefed before you came out, but it's different once you actually come here. I'm a full-time army nurse and this is my third tour. Don't worry, we're perfectly safe here. The hospital has never come under attack and even if it did, we're well protected. We nurses all take turns working between Resus, ITU and the wards. Your background is casualty, if I'm not mistaken?'

Tiggy nodded. 'Eight years in a busy city-centre A and E. I've seen most things.'

Sue smiled wryly. 'But not, I'm afraid, anything like you'll see here. And it's not just the soldiers, we get civilians too. Anyone who needs us, we patch 'em up before sending them on. The soldiers go to a military hospital in Germany or the UK; civilians we transfer to their local hospital.'

Tiggy's head was beginning to reel. Not for the first time, she wondered if she'd cope. What if one of her brothers was brought in? But then, that was why she was here. Even if, pray God, they didn't get injured, she would be able to help someone else's brother.

Sue paused in front of an open door. Inside, a group of men and women sat around joking and drinking tea and coffee.

'That's the team,' Sue said, 'a mixture of lifers, like me, and volunteers.'

Tiggy's eyes were immediately drawn to a man sitting in the centre of the group. Nick. He was laughing at something someone had said. Then he looked up and caught her eye. He pursed his lips in a soundless whistle and let his eyes roam over her body before dropping one eyelid in a wink. Whether it was the weather or something else, Tiggy felt heat race across her skin. In the dim light of the descending plane last night, she hadn't noticed just how gorgeous he was with his toffee-coloured eyes, weather-beaten face and high sharp cheekbones.

There was something about him that was sending warning signals to Tiggy's overheated brain. Danger and excitement radiated from him—along with a casual self-assurance, as if he was used to women gawping at him and almost expected it.

She tore her eyes away. Men like him were so out of her league. And even if he wasn't, he wasn't her type. When she fell in love it would be with a decent, steady, one-hundred-per-cent monogamous man. The only type who asked her out. Not that she had managed to fall for one of those, come to think of it.

Sue tapped her on the arm and grinned at her. 'Major Nick Casey—our very own playboy doctor.' She dropped her voice. 'Let me give you a word of warning. He eats woman like you for breakfast. If you want to survive with your heart intact, keep away from him. Trust me.' Her lips twitched. 'I've known Nick for a while and picked up the pieces of his conquests' broken hearts too often to count.' Sue's grin widened. 'Thankfully I'm married and immune to his charms.'

Nick stood and held out a chair, indicating with a tilt of his head that Tiggy should take it. Acutely conscious of his eyes on her, every step of the dozen or so required felt like a mile.

'Everyone, this is our latest, crazy volunteer, Lieutenant Tiggy Williams—otherwise known as Casualty Nurse Extraordinaire,' Sue introduced her with a flourish.

Tiggy knew she would no more get used to being called 'Lieutenant' than she would get used to the army revolver she had in her possession. It was beyond her why they had issued her with one. There wasn't the remotest chance of her ever firing it. She was more likely to shoot herself in the foot.

'Good to have you with us.' Nick grinned at her. His accent, like Sue's, was an unusual mixture of Irish and Scottish.

Her heart did a crazy pirouette and it took all her willpower not to whimper. She managed a cool smile—at least, she hoped it was a cool smile and not a grimace—in his direction before turning to hear the names of the folk with whom she'd be working closely over the coming months.

Apart from the surgeons, there were nurses, radiographers, physios and several other professionals all involved in making sure casualties had access to the best care. The names were too many for Tiggy to remember, but she felt reassured by the warmth of her colleagues' welcome.

'If you need anything, let us know,' an older nurse called Pat said. 'There's hardly any of us women so we have to stick together. Don't mind this lot, I keep them in order.'

Nick detached himself from the desk he'd been leaning on and loped towards Tiggy. Everyone was too busy catching up with one another to notice him bending his head and whispering in her ear.

'You recovered from the flight to hell yet?' His warm breath fanned her neck causing goose-bumps to spring up alarmingly all over her body. She much preferred it when he was way over on the other side of the room.

'Completely.'

'Good. You may have to go out in the 'copter sometimes, though, on a retrieval. You do know that?'

Although Tiggy had heard it might be a possibility that she'd be asked to accompany the medical emergency response team, she hoped to hell it wouldn't happen. If last night's flight had been scary, how much worse would it be going into an actual hot zone? She lifted her chin. 'If I'm needed, of course I'll go. I'm here to do my bit, the same as everyone else.'

'Good girl.' He straightened and once again Tiggy was aware of his eyes sweeping over her body.

'Hey, do you play poker?' one of the male nurses asked. 'I need someone new to take some money from. With the exception of Nick here, no one else will play with me any more.'

As everyone laughed, Nick turned towards them. 'Time for ward rounds. Let's go.'

They all started to troop away, leaving Tiggy feeling like a spare part. Nick fell back and touched her elbow.

'What's up, Red?'

If there was one thing Tiggy didn't like it was being teased about her hair. She had put up with twenty-six years of it from her brothers and she was damned if she would put up with it from him.

'The name's Tiggy,' she said through clenched teeth.

As Nick's grin widened, dimples appeared on either side of his mouth and her overactive heart skipped another beat. Why did he have to be so damned sexy?

'You'll find out everyone here has a nickname,' he drawled, and ruffled the hair on top of her head. 'Come on, follow me.'

Had he actually done that? Ruffled her hair? Like she was his kid sister?

She raised her hand to her curls in a vain attempt to restore some order. She had cut her hair into its current pixie style hoping it would make it more manageable, but the heat of the desert had its own ideas and she knew her fringe was curling.

She nibbled her lip. Why the hell was she fretting about how she looked? Just because she'd be working with a hunk it was no reason to be fretting about a curling fringe. And hunk or not, he clearly thought he was God's gift to women and, by the looks of it, probably tried it on with every new arrival. On the other hand, what did she have to worry about? Someone like him was bound to go after tall blondes with sylph-like figures—not curvy redheads with freckles.

She stared after his retreating back. Why, then, did the realisation give her no pleasure?

There were four patients between the two wards. In the first were three soldiers who, Sue explained, were in for observation and rehydration after a nasty bout of gastro-enteritis. 'We don't keep the injured men here for long. We patch them up, operate if we have to, then we pack them off to the Queen Elizabeth in Birmingham as soon as they're stable. You'll find that nursing here is a mixture of frenzied activity followed by hours of boredom.'

Sue introduced her to the patients while Nick read their notes. After he'd ordered more tests he spent a few minutes chatting with them, teasing them a little for shirking. Then they moved to the next ward.

Its only occupant was a little Afghan girl with masses of dark curls and round brown eyes who was sitting up in bed looking lost and scared. Her body, from her forehead to the top of her pyjama bottoms, was covered in red angry welts and her right arm was heavily bandaged.

'This is Hadiya,' Sue said with a smile at the little girl. 'She knocked over the family's paraffin heater a few days ago and sustained severe burns to her face, neck, chest and arm. We managed to save the arm, but she's going to require extensive reconstructive surgery if she's to regain full use of it.'

Nick said something in Pashto and the little girl giggled. All at once some of the fear left her eyes and she looked up at Nick with adoration.

'The surgeons had to remove a great deal of tissue from her hand and arm,' Sue continued, 'but she needs grafts.'

'The problem is,' Nick said slowly, 'we can't do it for her. Now she's stabilised she has to go to a local hospital and it's highly unlikely she'll get the surgery she needs there.'

'Why can't we do it here?' Tiggy asked.

'Because this is a military hospital and the reality is, if we make an exception for one civilian, how do we say no to others? Our resources would soon be overwhelmed. As difficult as it is, we have to transfer non-combative cases once they have stabilised.'

'But that's not right!'

Nick raised an eyebrow. 'What would you have us do?'

'I don't know! Something.'

He eyed her thoughtfully. 'I haven't given up on her if that's what you're thinking. In the meantime, however, we have other patients to see.'

CHAPTER TWO

How ANYONE COULD expect her to run around the perimeter of the camp in this heat while carrying a rucksack that weighed more than her own body weight, Tiggy couldn't imagine. It wasn't as if she was ever going to go out on patrol. That was left to the regular army doctors and the medics.

Although it was only just after six, the sun was already beating down and making her skin sizzle. She gasped for breath. If they didn't let her stop soon she was going to have a heart attack.

'Okay. Drop to the ground and give me twenty press-ups,' the sadistic sergeant shouted. Twenty! She doubted she could manage more than five. If that.

She didn't so much drop to her knees as collapse in a heap.

She had just finished her fourth press-up and was lying face down with her forehead resting on her hands when someone grabbed the back of her trousers and lifted her six inches off the ground.

'I believe you have a few more to go,' a familiar voice said. She didn't have to turn her head to know it was Nick, and that he was laughing.

She tried to wriggle out of his grasp but it was no use. The grip he had on the waistband of her trousers was such that she couldn't even turn far enough to see his face. 'Let me go,' she hissed.

'The sergeant isn't going to let up until you finish.'

As she was bobbed up and down she turned her head to the side. Sure enough, everyone else had finished and were all, including the traitorous Sue, sitting back on their haunches, taking long swigs from their water bottles and watching the scene with evident glee.

'Sixteen, seventeen,' Nick called out, and to Tiggy's added chagrin he was joined by several voices.

'Eighteen!'

Was this nightmare ever going to end? She took her mind off what was happening by imagining what she would do to Nick when she got the chance. Diuretics in his coffee? No, this needed something worse.

'Nineteen! Twenty!' He let her go so unexpectedly she sprawled face down in the dust. She staggered to her feet and furiously patted the dust from her front.

Nick held out his water bottle. 'You might need a drink.'

'If you ever—and I mean ever—do that to me again,' she snarled, 'I'll…'

He folded his arms and raised an eyebrow. 'Do what?'

She drew herself up to her full height and pushed away the water bottle. She wouldn't give him the satisfaction. 'Try it again, and you'll see.' God! Was that the best she could manage?

Then, unbearably conscious of everyone's eyes on her, she stalked away with as much dignity as she could muster.

Later, after she rinsed as much of the sand from her hair as she could in the dribble that passed for a shower, she went to report for duty, pausing only to pick up a banana from the mess.

She was still livid with Nick. Okay, so she might have

poured out her life story—or at least the first half of it—
to him while they had been on the plane, but that was no
reason for him to treat her like an annoying kid sister. Hell,
she was twenty-six.

And she didn't want Nick to treat her like a kid sister.

The thought brought her up short. Damn, she was no
better than the rest of Nick's admirers. But she had one
card up her sleeve. At least *she* knew he couldn't be taken
seriously. Her brother Charlie had been just like Nick. He
too had thought he was God's gift to women, having had
a seemingly endless series of short-term girlfriends until
he'd met and married Alice. Her other brother, Alan, was
still working his way through the female population of
the UK.

To her dismay, Nick was standing outside the main tent
when she arrived, almost as if he'd been waiting for her.
He had a cup of coffee in his hand.

'Recovered?' he asked.

'Very amusing. You've had your fun, now why don't
you go…' she waved her hands vaguely in the direction
of the camp '…and do some weightlifting or something?'

Dark eyes studied her and a small smile played on his
lips. 'Don't be mad,' he said softly.

'I don't get mad. I get even.'

She groaned inwardly. Couldn't she have thought of
a retort that was a little less clichéd? She was becoming more inarticulate by the minute. At least it was better
than blushing.

'Look,' she said, 'I know you're a major and I'm only
a lieutenant, but I won't be made a fool of.'

That was better! Now she was showing some backbone.

He lost the smile, although there was still a suspicious
glint in his eyes. 'You're right.' He raised his hand to his
head in a mock salute. 'I apologise. Unreservedly.'

Flustered by his unexpected apology, she looked at her watch. Seven-thirty. 'Don't you have work to do?'

He tossed the dregs of his coffee onto the ground. 'Actually, I don't. I've finished rounds and it's all quiet.' He eyed her speculatively. 'Don't suppose you play poker?'

'As a matter of fact, I do. However, unlike you, *I* have work to do.' She swept past him, aware that he was following her. Every hair on her body stood to attention.

'What about tomorrow? When you're finished for the day? Come over to the bar—the NCOs', that is. It has, let's just say, a more relaxed atmosphere there.'

Why was he so interested in what she did in her spare time? Why couldn't he just leave her alone? If he wanted someone to amuse him there were bound to be plenty of others happy to fill that role. However, a plan was forming in her mind. She turned around and smiled. 'Sure. Why not? Let's say six.'

Determined never to have a repeat of the fiasco with the press-ups, Tiggy decided to run around the camp perimeter every morning before breakfast. Despite the humiliation of having hundreds of men calling out encouragement as she wheezed and puffed her way around the track, she gritted her teeth and kept telling herself that she could do it. Anything was better than yesterday's embarrassment of having Nick's hands on the waistband of her trousers when he'd helped her complete her press-ups.

But once again, damn the man, he appeared like the devil from hell beside her. He shortened his strides to keep pace with her.

'Hello, Red. Turned over a new leaf, have you?'

'If you call me Red again,' she wheezed, 'so help me, I won't be responsible for my actions.'

A slow smile crossed his face. He held up his hands

with his fingers crossed. 'I promise never to call you Red again. If I do, you can have all my poker matches and that's a promise.'

She hid a smile. She hadn't known she could smile and run at the same time. He turned round so that he was running backwards. He was shirtless and his combat trousers were so low on his hips she couldn't help but notice his six-pack. She averted her eyes, pretending an interest in a passing Jeep.

'How many circuits?' he asked.

'This is my last.' She wasn't about to tell him it was also her first. One circuit was torture enough and she was determined to wait until she got to the safety of her quarters before she collapsed.

'I'm impressed.' His toffee-coloured eyes crinkled at the corners.

'Don't you have lives to save or something?' She indicated the hospital tent with her arm.

'Not right at the moment.' Even running backwards, he managed to look her up and down. 'I saw you come out for your run and the thought struck me that I might have to save yours. Looks like exercise hasn't exactly been high on your agenda until now.'

Was he implying she looked like a couch potato?

'Although you clearly do something to keep in shape,' he added.

Oh, please. Despite everything, the look of frank admiration in his eyes made her heart skip a beat.

Come on, Tiggy. Get a grip. This man is out of bounds and even if he wasn't, he is so not your type.

But it was as if her mouth had a mind of its own. 'Been watching me, huh?' A stitch had started somewhere below her ribs and the last word came out more as a cry of anguish than the casual reference she'd meant it to be. How long could one kilometre be? It could be the damned end of the world as far as she was concerned.

She gasped for air, trying to ignore the increasing pain in her side.

His eyes flickered over her and he frowned. 'You all right?'

'Never been better—or at least I will be when you leave… me…alone…' She managed another couple of strides and then had to stop. She bent over, clutching her knees, as a wave of pain slammed into her. Dear God, was she having a heart attack?

Before she knew it she was being lifted over his shoulder.

'Put me down,' she yelled into his back—a back that she couldn't help noticing, even from her upside-down position, was ridged with muscle.

'I will as soon as I find some shade. Don't you know better than to exercise in this heat? Are you crazy, woman? You should have started earlier, or there's a decent air-conditioned gym on the other side of the camp that's better suited for someone who's not used to exercise.'

There was a gym? An air-conditioned gym? Why on earth had no one told her? Why hadn't she asked?

Then she was inside her tent and he was laying her on the bed. Sue rushed over, concern furrowing her brow. 'What happened? Is she okay? Tiggy, speak to me.'

'I'm fine. Just need some water.' Sue held a bottle to her lips and she gulped thirstily.

'What have you been doing to the poor girl, Nick?' Sue demanded.

'Hey, don't blame me. I was just an innocent bystander.'

'Come off it! You've never been innocent or a bystander in your life!'

Nick laughed. 'Make sure she cools down before she goes on duty.' He leaned over and ruffled her hair. 'Stick to the gym in future.'

Later that afternoon, Tiggy studied the cards in her hand and suppressed a smile. Although every muscle ached, including some she hadn't known she had, her mood was improving.

She tossed a matchstick onto those already on the table. 'I'll raise you ten.'

Nick lifted an eyebrow. He counted out some matchsticks from his pile and added them to hers. They'd no casualties that day and Tiggy had spent most of her day with Hadiya, re-dressing her burns and being taught some words of Pashto by the little girl and her giggling mother. When the patients had all been seen to they'd set up a temporary poker table, at Nick's suggestion, in an empty cubicle. Some of the nurses and technicians had started off playing, too, but after two hours Nick and Tiggy were the only ones left in the game.

The rest of the team was either watching them play, flicking through magazines or answering the occasional call from the patients.

Nick wasn't to know, of course, that she played most nights with her father and her brothers whenever they were at home.

'Twenty and I'll see you.'

Nick leaned back in his chair and grinned. He placed his hand face up on the table. 'A flush! Beat that!'

Tiggy pretended to look dismayed, studying his cards as if she couldn't quite believe her bad luck. Then she allowed herself a small smile before laying hers down. 'Think my four aces beats your flush.'

Nick laughed. 'Beaten by a girl! Who would have thought? You have some poker face there, Red.'

She glared at him but before she could say anything he smiled and corrected himself. 'Apologies. Not Red, Tiggy.'

She blushed. She wished she managed her poker face as well in her private life.

At that moment the siren sounded.

'Two men down and possibly civilian injuries forty klicks away,' Sue interpreted the cackle from the radio. 'They're requesting a rapid medical response team to go in and bring them out.'

Nick had stood and was shrugging himself into his flak jacket. 'I need a nurse—any volunteers?'

'I'll go,' Tiggy said.

'No way,' Nick replied tersely. 'Anyone else?'

Irritated and relieved in equal measure, Tiggy glared at him. He didn't even seem to notice.

There was a show of hands and Nick picked an older man. 'Okay, Scotty, you're with me. The rest of you pre-pare to receive the casualties. I'll let you know what to expect as soon as I've made an assessment. Those who aren't needed and haven't donated recently, please give blood—just in case. Sue, turf out anyone from the wards who doesn't absolutely have to be there.' He grabbed his helmet and strode out of the room.

Instantaneously, everyone exploded into action. Sue, remembering Tiggy was there, propelled her towards the resus room. 'We need to make sure we have everything ready. At this stage we don't know what to expect or how much blood we'll need. What group are you?'

'O positive.'

'Perfect. One of the medics will get you started on a line.'

'Can't I help prepare for the casualties?'

Sue hesitated. 'We need your blood more than we need you right now. Don't worry, you'll get your fair share of action before your time here is up. In the meantime, watch and learn.'

When Sue was satisfied everything was ready for the incoming casualties, she came to check up on Tiggy.

She eyed the bag of blood. 'Another ten minutes max.'

While she'd been waiting for the bag to fill with her blood, Tiggy had been thinking about the little Afghan girl. She hoped Nick hadn't included her in his instructions to clear the ward.

'What about Hadiya?' she asked Sue. 'We're not going to discharge her too?'

Sue shook her head. 'Nick wants to keep her in for a bit.'

'But are we really going to send her away without further surgery?'

'It can't be helped.'

'Surely Nick can make an exception?'

Sue sighed. 'Believe me, if he could he would. And I haven't given up hope that he won't. If anyone can make a miracle happen, it's Nick. Now, I'd better get on. You just relax.'

Tiggy had finished giving blood, although Sue had insisted that she stay lying down afterwards. Frustrated, she watched as everyone double-checked that everything was ready. The radio crackled again and the staff paused to listen.

'We have two soldiers with shrapnel wounds. One has an injury to his left arm, the other abdominal wounds.' Nick's voice was calm over the roar of the helicopter's engines. 'ETA five minutes.'

The surgeon in charge of receiving the casualties turned

to his team. 'It sounds as if we'll need both theatres. Everyone to your stations.'

Tiggy eased herself up from the gurney and grabbed a leftover biscuit from the coffee table where everyone had been sitting. Although she still wasn't hungry, she knew she had to eat something. She was damned if she was going to stand by while everyone else around her worked, and fainting wouldn't endear her to anyone. Slipping into the changing room, she found a clean pair of scrubs and changed quickly. Her throat was still dry but she knew it wasn't from dust this time.

Before she could find Sue, the doors burst open and Nick entered, along with a couple of soldiers pushing a trolley. Nick was kneeling on top of his patient, doing chest compressions.

'He stopped breathing in the 'copter, but CPR has been given continuously. We've given him two units of red cells and two litres of colloid en route. We need to get him to Theatre stat.'

Willing hands stepped forward and rushed the patient through to Resus. Moments later, Scotty and more soldiers burst through the swing doors with the other stretcher.

'This man has shrapnel wounds to his arm,' Scotty called out. 'I've applied a temporary dressing and started a drip. Vital signs all okay.'

The injury to the second soldier's hand was such that for a moment Tiggy couldn't move.

As he too was wheeled into Resus, her training kicked in. She grabbed a pair of scissors and started cutting away the soldier's uniform, only vaguely aware of the staff crowded around the other patient, shouting orders.

Sue wheeled the portable X-ray over to Tiggy's patient. There was another flurry of activity as the soldier with the abdominal wound was taken into Theatre.

Nick crossed over to them, peeling off his gloves. Tiggy handed him a fresh pair. The soldier's vitals were getting worse. His blood pressure was dropping and his pulse becoming increasingly rapid and weak.

'We need to get his arm off. It's the only way to stop the bleeding,' the orthopaedic surgeon said, examining the wound.

'Let's try and stop the bleeding first, shall we?' Nick said quietly. 'The hand might not be salvageable, but we might be able to save his lower arm.'

'You have five minutes,' the orthopod said. 'After that, he's going to Theatre.'

They did everything they could to stop the bleeding, pumping the soldier with blood, but when Nick, along with the other surgeon, looked at the X-ray of the soldier's injury, he sighed, his eyes bleak. 'The damage is too bad,' he said. 'You're right, Simon. Amputation is the only way to go.'

Before she could help herself, a small cry escaped from Tiggy's lips. 'Are you sure? Isn't there anything we can do?'

Nick and Sue were already preparing the casualty for Theatre. 'If there was, we would do it,' Nick said tightly.

Tiggy swallowed hard. The boy was so young. But she knew Nick was right. The X-ray was there for them all to see, and Nick had already taken a chance by not sending the lad to Theatre straight away.

Nick looked at Tiggy and if she had any doubts as to how much he'd hoped to save the soldier's arm they vanished when she saw the anguish in his eyes. 'I promised these boys we would get them home and that's what we're going to do. I'll assist, Simon.'

Moments later, the resus room was empty.

* * *

Much later, when Dave, the soldier whose arm had been amputated, was settled on the ward, Tiggy escaped outside. She tried to control the tremors that kept running through her body.

'You okay?' Nick's voice came from behind her.

'No. Yes. I will be.' She took another deep breath. 'He's so young to lose an arm.'

'He'll learn to live without it.'

She whirled around. 'How can you say that? You don't have the remotest idea what it will be like for him.'

Nick's expression didn't change. 'No, you're right. I don't. If I lost my arm or the use of any of my limbs, I don't know what I'd do. But at least he's alive. At least he won't be going home in a body bag. Not like his colleague.'

They had been unable to save the other casualty. They all felt his loss as if he'd been their brother, their husband. When Nick had told them, his expression hadn't changed, and Tiggy wondered if she'd imagined his anguish earlier.

'How can you be so...' she sought for the right word '...unaffected?'

'Because they need me to be professional. They need us *all* to be professional.' Nick's voice was flat.

Tiggy slumped against the wall and wiped a hand across her perspiring brow. He was right, of course he was. If he could have saved the soldier's arm, he would have. Wishing otherwise wouldn't help anyone, least of all Dave.

She thought about her brothers. God help them all if either didn't make it. She couldn't even begin to imagine how her own mother would react. She loved her children with a tiger-like ferocity. Without warning, tears sprang to her eyes and she blinked furiously. She just couldn't help herself. It was too awful.

'Hey, Tiggy. Don't do that. Dave will be okay.' It was

the first time outside work she'd seen him look serious. 'We make it our job to get these boys back home alive, and mostly we do.' His eyes darkened. 'God, don't you think I hate not being able to send that boy home in one piece?'

'It's not just him—or the man who died. It's all of them. They're so young. And my brothers—they're out there, too.'

'There will be another team doing the same for them if they ever need help.'

Tiggy dabbed at her eyes with a tissue. 'I can't bear to think of them hurt.'

Nick reached out a hand and touched her shoulder. 'Most soldiers make it home, Tiggy,' he said. 'You have to hold on to that.'

She nodded, not trusting herself to speak.

He took her by the arm and steered her across the dusty strip of land in front of the hospital. 'Let's walk.'

'I'm not sure I can after this morning,' she said. Nevertheless, she allowed him to lead her across to the far side of the camp. A gentle breeze stirred the dust of the camp, cooling the intense night air. Above them a thousand stars studded the crystal clear sky. How could a place so beautiful hold so much heartache? When they reached a flat rock, Nick indicated with a nod of his head that they should sit. For a while they remained silent. Eventually Nick turned to her and grinned.

'So, Tiggy, the last I recall we were up to when you were thirteen. Why don't you tell me the rest?'

Later that week Tiggy was sitting outside her tent, drinking coffee with Sue. Across the camp men, most stripped to their combat trousers, were playing football or working out. Thankfully there had been no more life-threatening injuries to deal with. Dave had been transferred to the military hospital in Birmingham.

As a bare-chested soldier jogged past them, Sue grinned.

'You see? It's not all bad out here. Where else would you get the chance to ogle so many fit guys?'

'I can almost see the testosterone,' Tiggy admitted. Her eyes drifted over to Nick, who was pulling himself up on a bar suspended between two walls. He too was stripped to his combat trousers and the muscles in his naked back bunched every time he raised himself. Some soldiers sat in a circle, counting off every time he pulled himself up.

Sue followed the line of her gaze. 'As I said, forget him. He might be a hero but he's a woman's worst nightmare. As soon as he gets the girl he's been chasing, he loses interest. There's hardly a female on the camp—or off it for that matter—who hasn't had her heart broken by him.'

'You don't have to worry on that score. Nick might be a fine doctor, but his type has never appealed to me.'

Sue groaned. 'Don't say that! If he sees you're not interested, that will only make him worse.'

'I doubt I'm any more his type than he is mine, so you can rest easy.'

Sue eyed her speculatively. 'I would say you're just his type.' She drained her coffee mug.

Something Sue had said was niggling at the back of Tiggy's mind. 'Hey, before you go, what do you mean about Nick being a hero?'

Sue hesitated before sitting back down. 'Well, I guess I should tell you, although I'm surprised you haven't heard the story already.' Sue looked across at Nick. 'It was last year. Nick was out on an op with the men. They were making sure that a deserted village wasn't being used as a base for insurgents. It was a joint op with the Americans.

'Anyway, they got to the place—they call it a sangar—

where they were going to base themselves for the couple of weeks they expected the mission to last when fighting broke out. To cut a long story short, Nick left the safety of the sangar and, despite being fired on, ran to the aid of an injured man who had been dragged into one of the houses.'

'Good God!' Tiggy glanced across at Nick with new respect. So he wasn't just a playboy? Of course she already knew he was a great doctor but this latest revelation was making her assess him all over again.

Sue half smiled. 'That wasn't the end of it, though. While he was treating the American, one of his fellow soldiers came looking for him and took shrapnel to his upper thigh—straight into his femoral artery.'

Tiggy knew what that meant. The soldier wouldn't have stood a chance so far away from a proper medical facility.

'Poor sod.'

Sue rolled her empty mug between her hands. 'That's just it. He made it. And all because of Nick. Incredibly, Nick managed, while under fire and with the enemy practically at the door, to clamp off the artery. Thankfully he'd called in the medevac 'copter and God knows how but they managed to land close enough to get Nick and the injured man on board. Nick kept him alive until they made it back to camp. You can imagine how slim the soldier's chances of survival were—never mind keeping his leg—but Nick refused to give up. Somehow, he and the rest of the team were able to save the soldier's life and also salvage his leg.

'Since that day he's become a bit of a hero around here—and, believe me, there are no shortage of heroes in a place like this—as well as a talisman. The men believe that as long as Nick is with them, or as long as he's here on camp, they'll be all right. Sometimes I think they've invested him with supernatural powers.'

Perhaps that went some way to explaining Nick's arrogance, the air of total confidence surrounding him like an aura. She only hoped to hell there would be someone like him around if ever her brothers needed help.

'I had no idea,' Tiggy said softly.

'It's not something he goes around telling people.' Sue glanced at her watch. 'Time to get to bed.' When she looked back at Tiggy, her eyes were bleak. 'He might be a hero to the men but I think it's also a burden. Nick isn't a miracle-worker. He's human. I sometimes wonder if he hasn't started to believe his own legend.'

'And what's that?' Tiggy asked, rising too.

'Believing he's indestructible. And that as long as he's here, he can save everyone who has a chance.'

Tiggy's eyes strayed back to Nick. He had finished showing off and had picked up a towel and was wiping the sweat from his chest. Some six-pack, Tiggy thought distractedly. At that moment he looked up, and catching her staring at him, winked.

Tiggy blushed.

'Oh, dear,' Sue said. She picked up her mug again. 'Don't tell me I didn't warn you. See you at six.'

CHAPTER THREE

Nine years later

TIGGY RAN DOWN the hospital corridor with her heart in her mouth. A woman pushing an elderly man in a wheelchair flattened herself against the wall to make room for her to pass while a doctor, talking into her mobile phone, looked at her with sympathy.

Had a corridor ever seemed so long? Would she make it in time? What if his condition had deteriorated while she'd been on her way? What if he died before she had a chance to see him? A sob caught in her throat.

She skidded to a halt in front of the triage desk. Damn, damn, damn, there was a queue. She spun around, wondering whether she should risk slipping into Resus uninvited, but just then a doctor spotted her and came over.

'Mrs Casey?' he asked. 'I'm Dr Luke Blackman. It was me who called you.' She had already guessed that as soon as he'd started to speak. She recognised his voice straight away.

Today had started like any other day. She'd been off duty when the phone had rung. At first the American accent on the other end of the line had thrown her. Then, when the male voice had identified himself as a doctor from the Royal London, her first panicked thought had been that something had happened to Alan, who was still flying Apaches in Afghanistan. But it was Nick he was calling about. Nick had been brought into the hospital with a head wound and was asking for her.

Without waiting to hear any more, she'd dropped the phone and bolted for her car.

She searched Dr Blackman's face, trying to read his expression for clues, but his calm exterior gave nothing away. 'Why don't we go into the relatives' room? It will give us some privacy.'

She felt sick. People were usually invited into the relatives' room so they could be given bad news.

'Just tell me.' Her lips were so numb she could barely articulate the words. 'Is he dead?'

'Dead?' Dr Blackman's mouth relaxed into a smile. 'No the lieutenant colonel is very much alive. He was drifting in and out of consciousness for a while but he's going to be just fine.'

Relief buckled her knees. Still, she had to see Nick for herself.

'Take me to him,' she said.

'I think we should talk first.'

Tiggy straightened to her full five feet five. Whatever Dr Blackman had to tell her could wait. 'Please, Doctor, I need to see him. Now.'

The doctor clearly realised she was in no mood to be thwarted. 'Very well. If you'll follow me?'

Nick was lying on his bed, as still and as white as a corpse. His head was bandaged and there was a dark bruise on his left cheekbone only partly hidden by the stubble of his unshaven face.

But it was still Nick. Her husband. The man she hadn't seen for six years.

* * *

Nick's head was filled with images. Bombs were exploding, helicopter blades whirled incessantly, scattering dust
everywhere. There was blood, so much blood, and soldiers
and civilians running in panic. Then someone was stick-
ing something into his arm.

Slowly the nightmare scenes began to fade and a strange
sense of calm filled him as Tiggy's face appeared before
him; her blue eyes were wide, her red hair a sharp contrast to the paleness of her skin. The vision shifted and he
was holding her, kissing her——she was in his bed, in his
arms, laughing up at him, giggling at something he'd said.

He liked it when he dreamt of her.

'I'm here, Nick,' he heard her saying in that quiet, determined way she had. 'Everything's going to be all right.'
Her voice was like cool rain on a hot night. Even in his
nightmares the memory of her voice, her touch, always
soothed him. It was when he was awake that the memory
of her tormented him.

'Can you hear me, Nick?' a different voice said. An
American, by the sound of him.

'Come on, Nick. You need to open your eyes.' It was
Tiggy speaking again. Much better. He far preferred her
voice to the American's. But he was damned if he was
going to wake up. The dream was so much better.

'Nick, for God's sake, say something!'

If he hadn't known he was dreaming, he would have
sworn it was Tiggy. But that was impossible. Tiggy was
lost to him. Well and truly lost, as he was damn well going
to tell that nagging voice.

He shifted slightly, trying to force his limbs to move.
God, his body was aching. It was as if he'd been driven
over by a Humvee. But he hadn't been run over by a military vehicle or anything else. He hadn't been in Afghani-

stan. He'd been in London. Other fragmented memories flooded back. The last thing he remembered was that he had been walking down a street. Which one he couldn't for the life of him recall. A man had been on the ground. Someone had been kicking him. He'd moved in to stop the fight. He'd taken a blow to his stomach, but not before he'd landed one of his own. After that? Nothing. Except an exploding pain in his head.

Using every ounce of willpower he could muster, he reluctantly opened his eyes.

He had to be still dreaming. Tiggy was bending over him, her beautiful eyes awash with tears. It couldn't be her. Not after all this time, and not after what he'd put her through. He closed his eyes again. Now, if only he could get back to the dream where she was lying in his arms, laughing up at him. He didn't like Tiggy being sad.

But damn. He was awake now. He opened one eye. The image of Tiggy was still there. He closed his eyes and opened them again. No, it was no hallucination. No dream. It was her.

'What the hell are you doing here?' he growled.

Tiggy reeled as if she'd been slapped. But what had she expected? That Nick would be pleased to see her? Considering the way they'd parted, it was as likely as a snowstorm in the desert. Yet when he'd first opened his eyes she could have sworn it had been hunger—and pleasure—she'd read in their brown depths. She had been wrong.

At least he wasn't dead. In fact, as Dr Blackman had said, he was very much alive.

She looked at Dr Blackman and raised her eyebrows.

'Lieutenant Colonel—Nick—this is your wife. You were asking for her. I found her details on your records and called her.'

'Not possible. Not married.'

Tiggy's throat tightened. Now she knew he was in one piece, she felt all her old anger resurface. She turned to the bemused-looking doctor.

'I should tell you that Nick and I are separated, and have been for six years.' Six long years, where every day at first had been a fight to get through it without him. And now, just when she'd thought he was out of her head and her heart, here he was, and, even unshaven and with his bruised cheek he still made her pulse leap.

God damn it.

Nick's hand snaked out from under the sheets and grabbed Dr Blackman by the arm. 'Who the hell gave you the right to call my ex-wife?'

It was on the tip of her tongue to point out that whatever he said, or wanted to believe, she wasn't actually his *ex-*wife. Although she'd always intended to, she'd never quite got around to signing the divorce papers. And neither had he. Clearly he hadn't removed her as his next of kin either.

'You were asking for a Tiggy when you came in. It was the same name listed on your record as next of kin. Of course we contacted her,' Dr Blackman replied, looking baffled.

Tiggy couldn't blame him. His patient had been calling out for a woman who was listed as his wife, yet the patient obviously couldn't bear the sight of her.

'I don't care if her name is up somewhere in lights. Get her the hell out of here.'

Tiggy's throat tightened. 'Don't worry, Nick, you don't have to ask me twice. I'm going.'

She turned on her heel and headed for the door.

She heard Dr Blackman tell Nick he'd be back to see him shortly then the doctor was by her side.

'Mrs Casey, don't take his reaction too much to heart.

The head injury is probably making him confused and irritable. I wouldn't put too much store in what he's saying now.'

She smiled tightly. 'Trust me, he's not confused. He knows exactly what he's saying. I shouldn't have come.' She glanced over towards the exit. She needed to get out of there.

'Look, I can see you're upset. Come into the staffroom. We can talk there.'

'Really, I don't think that's a good idea. Find someone else.' Her mouth twisted. 'I'm sure Nick has some woman in his life you should call. Why don't you ask him?'

'Please, Mrs Casey. It won't take long.'

Tiggy hesitated before nodding. Of course she couldn't leave. Not without knowing for certain he wasn't in any danger.

The thought almost made her laugh out loud. For years she'd been terrified something would happen to Nick in Afghanistan, and he'd had to come back to the UK for her worst fears to come true.

'What happened?' she asked when they were both seated.

'He was brought into A and E a few hours ago. There was a bit of a...' Dr Blackman looked as if he was struggling to find the right words '...er...scuffle. At the moment my main concern is with the injury to his head. I've scheduled him for a scan.' He leaned forward, his eyes curious. 'We'll know more once we have the results of all his tests.'

'What was he doing in a fight anyway?' she asked. Nick had always been impulsive and his behaviour had become increasingly erratic towards the end of their marriage, but a fight in the street? That didn't fit with what she knew of Nick. Had he been drinking? In the past he'd hardly touched alcohol. But a person could change in six years.

If she wanted any evidence of that, all she had to do was remember how much he'd changed in the three years they had been married.

Dr Blackman looked at her and smiled. 'I understand that LC Casey was breaking up a fight. Some thugs had a young man on the ground and were kicking him. LC Casey intervened.' His smile grew wider. 'He always was a hero.'

'You know Nick, Dr Blackman?'

'Please, call me Luke. Not really. We met ten years ago. I was with the forces back then. I've never forgotten him.'

She half smiled. Nick wasn't exactly forgettable. She of all people knew that.

Luke's pager bleeped and he paused to look at it. 'I'm sorry, I have to go. I'll contact you again when we have the results of the scan.'

As he rose, she stumbled to her feet and held out her hand, swallowing the hard lump in her throat. 'Thanks for calling me. Take good care of him.'

Nick gritted his teeth and, as instructed, squeezed Dr Blackman's hand as hard as he could.

Damn the doctor for contacting Tiggy. But he couldn't really blame him. He should have removed her as his next of kin years ago. The problem was there hadn't been anyone else to put down. But was that the only reason? Or was it that he hadn't been able to bring himself to sever his last ties with her, no matter how much he knew it was the right thing to do?

'You don't recognise me, do you?' The doctor took out his ophthalmoscope. 'I'm going to look in your eyes.'

'Should I?' Nick muttered. Why had Tiggy come anyway? Knowing her, it would be out of some misplaced sense of duty. He didn't want, or need, her sympathy.

'We met ten years ago. In Afghanistan. You saved my

life.' Dr Blackman shone his light in Nick's left eye. 'I was a soldier with the US Army back then.'

Immediately Nick was transported back to the deserted house and the soldier with the pumping femoral artery. He'd thought there was something familiar about the A and E doctor, but it hadn't crossed his mind that he was the same man he'd treated all those years ago.

'Good God! What are you doing here?'

The American straightened and flicked through Nick's notes. 'Didn't think I would end up a doctor?' He grinned. 'It's down to you that I am. Coming face to face with death is enough to make any man re-evaluate where he's going with his life.'

Nick remembered the scars on his chest, the tattoo. Not a man he would have ever expected to find in a hospital, let alone treating him.

'I owe it to you. Back then, well, let's just say I was set on a course to hell. As soon as I recovered I left the army and went to medical school. I'm here on an exchange fellowship.'

They had more in common than Luke could possibly know.

'How's the leg?' Nick asked.

'It's good. I limp a little when I'm tired, but apart from that...' Luke closed the case notes and studied Nick thoughtfully. 'I'm sure you're aware that you have some left-sided weakness. I see you had an injury to your spine a few years ago and that there was some shrapnel that the surgeons decided it was safer not to remove. I think we should do an MR scan.'

Nick shook his head. 'I don't think so.' The weakness was barely noticeable and certainly wasn't hindering his ability to do his job. But once people started poking around, who knew what would happen?

Luke folded his arms and returned his stare steadily. 'Lieutenant Colonel Casey, I want to thank you for saving my life and my leg. I always regretted that I never got a chance back then. But the best way I can thank you is by looking after you the best way I can.'

Nick raised himself on his elbows. 'If you really want to thank me, Doctor, get me the hell out of here.'

CHAPTER FOUR

THAT NIGHT TIGGY barely slept. It had been a shock seeing Nick in the hospital looking so helpless. He'd always been so alive—so vital. How could he have risked his life to save someone he didn't know? But that was Nick all over. He had always done whatever he needed to do to save the lives of his men—and damn the consequences. And wasn't that part of the reason she had fallen in love with him in the first place?

The day she'd realised she was falling in love with Nick was forever imprinted in her memory.

Back then there had still been a truce of sorts between the locals and the army and they hadn't been very busy. At least, not since the two badly injured soldiers had been brought in. In the weeks that had followed most of the patients they'd treated had been locals presenting themselves at the clinic with the same sort of injuries Tiggy had experienced in her A and E department: burns; broken bones; car accidents; as well as the usual bugs and infections. Every now and again there would be a shout and injured soldiers would be brought in requiring the staff's full attention, but in between there had been plenty of time off to socialise.

To her surprise, Nick had kept seeking her out, although

she had gone out of her way to avoid him. Then one day the team had been called out to a medevac case.

Nick was already putting on his flak jacket when Tiggy, early for her shift, arrived in the department.

'Where's Sue?' he asked.

'Still in the shower. Why?'

'Damn. The night staff are busy in Theatre or in the wards and I need a nurse to come on a retrieval. There's been some trouble in one of the villages. There might be multiple casualties.'

'I'll come.'

Nick shook his head. 'You're not regular army.'

'But I am a nurse.'

When Nick hesitated, Tiggy continued, 'The night shift are due to go off duty when they finish, and the day shift aren't on yet. However, I'm here, qualified and ready to go.'

'Going out to retrieve patients isn't part of your remit. I don't have time to argue, Tiggy.'

'In that case, don't.'

She picked up the nurse's bag and her flak jacket.

Nick frowned and glanced around as if he could conjure up a nurse out of thin air. Anyone but her. But not even he could do the impossible.

'Okay. But *don't* even *think* of getting off the 'copter. Understood?'

'Aye, aye, sir.' She grinned and saluted him.

But as reality sank in—she'd be going in a helicopter, for God's sake, and flying into a hot zone—her excitement was replaced with nauseating adrenaline. Luckily, before terror gripped her completely, she found herself in the back of the Chinook alongside Nick. He picked up a pair of noise defenders and, pushing her curls under her Kevlar helmet, placed them on her ears.

'We'll speak through the mike from now on. Only talk when you have something to say.'

Tiggy had been in a Chinook during training so she knew that the helicopter was fitted out like a mini casualty unit with everything they needed to keep a soldier alive until they got him back to base.

However, in training there hadn't been soldiers armed with machine guns hanging out the doors. She shuddered.

When they took off, the helicopter's nose pointed sharply downwards and for one horrified moment Tiggy thought it was going to plummet to the ground. She squeezed her eyes shut.

'You okay?' Nick's disembodied voice came through her earpiece.

She opened her eyes slowly and managed a nod.

He studied her. 'You're terrified of flying, yet you volunteered to come?'

'Not going to let it get the better of me,' she replied through gritted teeth.

He grinned and touched his helmet in a mock salute. He covered the mike with his hand and bent towards her. 'You're something else, you know that? You have some guts.'

'I'm bloody terrified,' she yelled back.

'Hey, don't you know that doing something when you're scared is the true test of bravery?'

He was right. She might be scared out of her wits but she was there. The realisation calmed her and somehow the flight wasn't so terrifying after that. Ten minutes later they were touching down.

'Stay here,' Nick said again, before leaping out of the helicopter and following the soldiers in a crouched position as they ran towards what once must have been a house and was now a pile of rubble.

After what seemed like hours but could only have been minutes, the soldiers returned with the casualty.

As the stretcher was lifted on board, Nick jumped in and the helicopter rose steeply and headed off back in the direction from which they'd come.

But the injured man wasn't a soldier. It was a young Afghan, who was bleeding from a head wound.

She hooked him up to the monitor and glanced at Nick.

'Head injury, Glasgow coma scale of seven,' she said quietly. 'Not good.'

'Where to, Major?' The pilot's voice came through the headphones. 'I'm assuming the local hospital?'

'No. Head for base,' Nick replied.

'Is that an order, sir?' the pilot said. 'You are aware that's contrary to standing instructions?' Tiggy knew it was standard practice to take civilian casualties to the local hospital, but they were badly equipped and under-staffed. This boy needed the expertise and resources he'd only get back at the camp.

'I know what the damn standing orders are,' Nick said tersely, 'but this man will die unless he's treated by us. While I'm on board, where we go is my decision.'

Tiggy sucked in a breath. Nick could be in deep trouble for disobeying orders.

He looked up and caught her eye. Unbelievably, he winked. 'Never have been one for doing what I'm told.' He grinned. 'Now, Nurse, let's do what we have to do to keep this man alive.'

And it was then, at that precise moment, that Tiggy knew. She was falling in love with Major Nick Casey.

CHAPTER FIVE

Thankfully, Paediatric A and E was quiet, with no more than a few colds and sniffles and the odd sprained or broken limb. For once, Tiggy worked on autopilot and somehow managed to get through her shift. She was just about to leave when one of the nurses held out the phone.

'Call for you. It's a Dr Blackman from the Royal London.'

Tiggy's heart froze. Had Nick relapsed? It was always possible after a head injury.

Her hands were shaking so badly she could hardly hold the phone.

'Mrs Casey,' Luke said, 'don't worry, the LC is not in any immediate danger, but I think it would be a good idea if we talked. He'd probably have my head if he knew I was contacting you again but, in my opinion, Nick is going to need all the help he can get.'

Tiggy closed her eyes. It was on the tip of her tongue to tell Dr Blackman to go to hell and take Nick with him. But of course she couldn't.

'I'll be there as soon as I can.'

Thirty minutes later she was sitting opposite Luke, trying to focus on what he was saying. Something about an operation…

'But Nick's okay?'

'Yes and no. He's up in the surgical ward. When we did the MR scan we discovered an old injury.'

'What kind of injury?'

'Two years ago, the LC was in a convoy when an IED exploded under the truck in front of him. He and his men managed to get out of their truck and the LC was going towards the injured men when the insurgents, who'd been waiting in a ditch by the side of the road, opened fire.'

Tiggy's mouth was so dry it felt as if her tongue was stuck to its roof. Was Nick determined to kill himself one way or another? 'What happened to him?'

'He took some shrapnel. He was wearing his Kevlar vest, otherwise he'd be dead for sure.'

'Oh, God!' Her heart catapulted at the thought of Nick being injured and her not even knowing.

'He was in Intensive Care for two weeks. But luckily, like most men in the army, he's as strong as an ox. Regular soldiers are so fit that if they survive the initial assault to their bodies they heal remarkably quickly. The LC seemed to make a full recovery.'

'Seemed? I'm afraid I don't understand.'

'There was a piece of shrapnel close to his spinal cord. To remove it could have caused paralysis. Where it was, it wasn't doing any harm, so the operating surgeons decided on balance to leave it.'

She shook her head. 'But why am I here? I think Nick has made it perfectly clear he doesn't want me involved in his care so I'm afraid you're going to have to spell it out.'

'The piece of shrapnel the surgeons left has moved. When he was in A and E we put him through the usual battery of neurological exams. Although he tried to hide it, we picked up some weakness in his left side. After we applied a little verbal pressure...' Luke frowned and Tiggy guessed it had to have been more than a little pressure '...the LC admitted that he started having headaches and some left-sided weakness a couple of months ago. I persuaded him to go for a scan. He was pretty reluctant, but eventually he agreed after I threatened to call the GMC if he didn't.'

Tiggy almost smiled. Nothing had changed. Nick had always been a law unto himself. 'So you're wondering whether to operate?'

'That's what I'm recommending, but he won't listen to me.' He sighed heavily. 'I thought you might be able to persuade him. I know I'm going out on a limb here, but I owe the LC big time. He saved my life, you know.'

Tiggy leaned forward. 'Tell me.'

'Ten years ago, I was a soldier in the US army. We were doing a joint manoeuvre with the British. Out of the blue everything went to hell. One of my buddies was hit. We were pinned down behind some walls and Brad was in one of the deserted houses. We knew he'd been hit, but nobody could get to him. We never leave a man down, so I thought I would fetch him.'

The smile he gave was fleeting and Tiggy knew there was a lot more he wasn't saying. 'LC Casey—he was Major Casey back then—was the platoon doctor with the Brits. I didn't know it, but he was already there with Brad.'

All at once, it came to Tiggy.

'You were the American with the bleeding femoral artery.'

'You know about that?'

'Not from Nick. He never spoke about it but he couldn't stop the story passing into camp folklore. I still don't see how I can help. Nick never listened to me in the past so I doubt he's going to start now. Besides, you saw how he was yesterday. He couldn't have made it clearer that he doesn't want me involved.'

Luke placed his elbows on his knees and leaned closer.

'I also heard the way he was calling for you when he was barely conscious. In my experience, nobody calls out for someone like that if they mean nothing.'

Nick calling for her didn't make sense. Apart from sending her the divorce papers to sign, Nick hadn't tried to contact her in six years. He'd walked away from her, and their marriage, as if she'd meant nothing.

'You have to try,' Luke continued. 'If we don't remove that shrapnel he could become completely paralysed. Worst-case scenario, he could die.'

Tiggy jumped to her feet and started pacing. Didn't Luke know what he was asking was a waste of time? She was the last person Nick would listen to.

'Does he know you've contacted me again?'

'No.' Luke's lips twitched. 'In fact, he told me if I did, he would make sure I never worked again. Or words to that effect.'

'Then I don't know what I can do. I wish I could help. But apart from yesterday I haven't seen my husband for six years.'

'Please, Mrs Casey. Give it a try at least.'

Tiggy sighed. Her insides felt like a washing machine. Of course she had to give it a try. Whatever had happened between Nick and herself, she couldn't sit back and do nothing.

She got to her feet. 'What are we waiting for?'

She picked him out straight away. He was playing cards with a group of men in the centre of the ward and his height meant that even sitting down he towered above the other men. She wondered if the game they were playing was poker. If it was, no doubt Nick would be fleecing his fellow patients.

As if he felt her presence, he looked up.

They'd removed the bandage from his head and now that he was up and no longer attached to monitors, she could get a proper look at him.

His hair was longer than when she'd last seen him and he had more lines than she remembered. Two deep grooves bracketed his mouth.

But it was his eyes that made her catch her breath. They were empty, almost entirely devoid of emotion. Whatever Luke said, whatever she'd imagined, Nick felt nothing for her, not any more.

A lump of ice took up residence in her chest.

Nick said a few words to his fellow card-players, stood up and started towards them. Although he was trying to hide it, he couldn't quite disguise his limp.

'What the hell are you doing back here?' he growled, glaring at her.

So her intuition had been right. Yesterday hadn't been an aberration. He didn't want to see her.

It took every ounce of her willpower not to back away from his fury. God only knew how, but she managed to keep her voice even. 'Hello to you too, Nick.'

He turned cold eyes on Luke. 'Did you contact her? Because I remember explicitly telling you that I refused to give my permission. I could have you up in front of the GMC for this.'

'I see a blow to the head hasn't changed you,' Tiggy said mildly, although her heart was beating like a drum against her ribs.

'I want you to leave,' Nick said flatly. Had this man ever looked at her as if she were the most precious thing in the world? 'In case you've forgotten, we're no longer married.'

'Actually, Nick, in case you've forgotten, we *are* still married. And I'm still your next of kin.'

His mouth settled into the hard, stubborn line she had

come to know so well. 'It doesn't matter what it says on a piece of paper I'm able to make my own decisions.'

'Why don't we all sit down?' Luke said, apparently oblivious to the tension that fizzed between them.

Looking capable of picking Tiggy up and carrying her outside himself, Nick reluctantly led the way across to his bed. When Tiggy went to help him, he shrugged her away.

'I'm afraid, Lieutenant Colonel,' Luke said, 'we're not convinced that you can make rational decisions. If you were, you'd see that an operation is essential.'

Nick turned the full force of his fury on Luke. 'I'd like a word with *my wife*,' he ground out, emphasising the last two words with heavy sarcasm.

Luke glanced from Nick to Tiggy as if he too wasn't sure of what Nick would do if left to his own devices. Then he shook his head. 'Sure. I have patients I want to look in on. I'll be back in a while.'

Nick waited until Luke was out of hearing. 'As I said, Tiggy, I don't want you here. My health is not your concern.'

Tiggy folded her arms. 'That's tough. I'm not going anywhere. God, Nick, why didn't you tell me you'd been badly injured? You were in Intensive Care and you didn't even let me know!'

But was she really surprised? Two years after they'd married Nick had stopped talking to her about the important stuff.

'What difference would it have made? Our marriage was—is—over.'

'I'm not likely to forget that,' she retorted. 'Look, Nick, I'm here now. Can't we at least be civil to each other?'

He glared at her but she refused to look away. Suddenly the grim line of his mouth softened and when he smiled she caught a glimpse of the Nick she had first known and her insides melted. 'Sorry. Of course.' He dragged a hand across the stubble on his cheek. 'Forgive me.'

As he turned away to take something from his locker, she studied him more carefully. He may have changed, but he still made her catch her breath. She still remembered the feel of him, remembered every inch of his body, the hard muscles of his abdomen, his long legs and powerful thighs, the feel of his fingertips on her skin, the planes of his face under hers. She bit back a groan and closed her eyes.

Six years, and he still made her pulse race. Six years since she'd seen him and one glance was enough for her to know she'd never got him out of her head. She should get the hell away from him—simply walk out the door. Not just walk—run as fast as her legs could carry her.

'Okay, now we've caught up, thanks for the visit.' Nick shifted in his seat. Clearly his leg was causing him some discomfort.

'It's started,' she said softly, 'hasn't it? The paralysis Luke was talking about. Oh, Nick...' He'd been a triathlete in the past and had always been so fit. She knew how much he'd hate not being in peak physical condition.

His eyes were cool. 'It's a little stiff, that's all. Comes from getting in a fight, I guess.'

'And as for fighting in the street, what were you thinking? They could have had knives. God, you could have been killed.'

Nick shrugged. 'Nothing else I could do.'

'You could have called the police. It's what any sane person would have done.'

Nick shook his head. 'And waited ten minutes for them to arrive? I could hardly stand around doing nothing while they kicked a man to death. Surely even you can see that?'

Of course she did. The Nick she knew would never

have stood back. Not even if the men had been armed to the teeth with guns as well as knives.

'Still playing the hero, then?' she said.

Wasn't his hero status part of his attraction? Why, even when she knew she was getting in too deep, she couldn't resist him? She closed her eyes, remembering the day she'd realised she was in love with him and that he had felt something for her too...

The time in the camp had passed quickly. When she hadn't been working she played poker with Nick and some of the others, using one of the resus beds as a table. In the evenings the staff who were off duty got together for drinks in the bar—although while it was called a bar, in camp only soft drinks had been served. Other nights there were plays, sometimes even concerts. A group of army medics had brought their instruments with them and often in the evenings she and Sue, along with the other nurses and doctors, would sit around and listen to them play.

Nick had invariably been there. The man had known more about her than anyone, apart from her own family. He'd seemed to *adopt* her as an honorary kid sister. Sometimes she would catch him looking at her and her heart would thump and she would have difficulty breathing. Despite everything she'd told herself, her reaction to him had been anything but that of a sister.

If Nick had been hauled over the coals for disobeying orders the day she'd accompanied him on the retrieval, she never found out. What she did know was that their young Afghan patient, who turned out to be only seventeen, went on to make a full recovery. Something that was unlikely to have happened in his local hospital.

And soon after that she discovered that Nick had arranged for Hadiya, the child with burns, to be flown to the UK, with her family, *for treatment*.

Everything she learned about him just made her fall for him a little deeper every day.

She'd been at the camp for four weeks when, after a late night listening to the band, she looked up to find him standing behind her.

He held out his hand. 'Come with me, Tiggy.'

She thought her heart would stop. Almost in a trance, she took his hand and allowed him to lead her away from the group and into the darkness.

'Where are we going?' she whispered.

'Somewhere away from prying eyes.'

Her heart pounding, she let him lead her to a quiet place behind one of the accommodation blocks. Suddenly he pulled her against him and kissed her.

His kiss was everything she'd imagined and more. And, God help her, she had been fantasizing about how it would feel to be in his arms. She'd been kissed before but likening Nick's kiss to her previous experiences was like comparing a single star to the Milky Way.

His mouth was hard and demanding, in a way that reminded her that he'd kissed a hundred women before her.

One hand was on her hip, pulling her close, the other was in her hair. His lean, muscular body felt just as good as she'd anticipated, and her very bones seemed to melt.

When he let her go she found it so difficult to breathe she thought she would hyperventilate.

'Do you know, I've wanted to do that since the first time I saw you?' he asked.

'You have?' she squeaked. *Oh, God*, couldn't she at least pretend to be more used to being kissed like that?

His eyes locked on hers. 'I don't know how I've managed to keep my hands off you until now.'

As he bent his head to kiss her again she came to her senses. Nick wouldn't be satisfied with just kisses. And she was damned if she would be his plaything. She placed her hands against his chest. She loved the feel of his muscles under her fingertips, which wasn't helping her resolve.

'Don't, Nick,' she managed.

'Why not? I know you liked me kissing you.' When he reached for her again, she stepped away.

'I'm not one of your conquests, Nick.' She lifted her chin. 'I have my pride.'

To her disbelief, he threw back his head and laughed. 'Tiggy, if you were just that, don't you think I would have made my move before now? Do you have any idea how difficult it's been for me to keep my hands off you, knowing that if I made my move too soon I'd scare you away?'

He'd been thinking of her, just as she'd been thinking of him? Warmth curled in her belly. Perhaps everyone was wrong about Nick…

Perhaps even Sue was wrong about Nick…

She sighed. Sue wouldn't have warned her off if she hadn't been sure *he* couldn't be trusted.

'Don't make fun of me, Nick. I'm not good at these kinds of games.'

His smile disappeared. 'Make fun of you? Don't you have any idea what you do to me, woman? I kept away from you not just because I didn't want to frighten you off but because of what you were doing to my head. No one has done this to me before.'

She wished she could believe him. If only wishes were horses, or whatever the expression was. But she wasn't so naive that she didn't know Nick was the kind of man to take whatever he wanted and to hell with the consequences.

'In that case,' she retorted, 'you're going to have to work hard to convince me that's true. In the meantime,

I'm going to bed.' And as his eyes glinted in the moon-light, she added. 'Alone. Goodnight, Nick.'

'Time for your medication, Nick.'

Tiggy was brought back to the present as a nurse with a perky smile appeared by the bedside.

Nick held out his hand and, taking the small plastic cup from the nurse's hands, tossed the tablets down his throat.

The nurse eyed Tiggy then looked back at Nick. 'I see we have visitors today.' Her glance at Tiggy wasn't ex-actly friendly.

'This is Tiggy. She's just leaving.'

Tiggy ignored him. Although every cell in her body was screaming at her to run, she knew she wasn't going any-where. Not until Nick had promised to at least consider the operation. After that he was on his own, and they could go back to acting like strangers instead of two people who had once loved each other more than she'd thought possible.

'I hope Dr Casey hasn't been giving you too hard a time,' Tiggy said to the nurse with a smile. 'He can be a little grouchy.'

The nurse giggled and blushed. 'No, not at all...'

Whatever else was wrong with Nick, it wasn't his flirt-ing skills.

Jealousy ripped through her, stealing her breath. How many women had he slept with since they'd separated? There were bound to have been several. It had been years after all.

Not that it was any concern of hers. Not any more.

All of a sudden she'd had enough. Her head felt as if it was about to explode. She had to get out of there.

She bent over Nick and took the plastic cup from his hands. She thought about kissing him on the cheek, but at the last moment decided against it. Knowing Nick, he would consider it a sign of possession.

'I'll be back this evening,' she said. 'We'll talk more then.'

Nick waited until the nurse had disappeared before shaking his head. 'Don't come back, Tiggy. Can't you get it into your head? You and I are nothing to each other any more. Haven't been for years. In fact, tomorrow I intend to call my lawyer and restart the divorce proceedings.'

Tiggy sucked in a breath. 'Very well,' she replied, glad her voice wasn't wobbling the way her heart was. 'You do that. But in the meantime I'm your next of kin. I'm coming back tonight. You can choose to ignore me if you want but, whether you like it or not, I am coming back.'

Nick watched Tiggy leave.

She was still beautiful. Thinner perhaps, and her hair was longer, but she still made his gut tighten.

He clenched his jaw. He still hated himself for the way he'd hurt her. Why had he married her in the first place? He should have known that he and Tiggy were never going to have a happy ever after.

But, God, he'd been in love. So much he'd thought it could work. If anyone could save his soul, he'd told himself, Tiggy could.

He'd been wrong. His soul wasn't salvageable. At least, not by someone like Tiggy. He'd tried to make her happy and in the first year of their marriage it had seemed he'd succeeded. He'd hated being away from her, but then... He shook his head. Being with her had become the thing that had torn him apart. So he'd done the only thing he could. The only honourable thing, even if it had been three years too late: he'd left her, knowing it was the only way that she would find the happiness she deserved.

She had moved on with her life so she had to be here out of a sense of duty or, even worse, pity. The thought made him cringe. He didn't need or want her pity.

He wanted her to look at him the way she used to.

Why was he thinking that way? That was the road to hell for both of them.

So now, more than ever, he needed to convince her to forget about him. Even though seeing her again was doing something to him he hadn't felt for a long, long time.

A nurse stopped by his bed and pulled the screens. 'Time for your nap, Nick.'

Time for his nap? Did she think he was a child? Hell. He needed to get out of here.

CHAPTER SIX

AS SOON AS Tiggy got home she changed into her running gear and, despite the rain soaking the earth, decided to go for a ten-mile run. She needed to exhaust herself if she wanted to stop thinking about Nick. Not for the first time she wondered what would have happened if she'd listened to Sue and kept well away from him. Of course, that would have been easier if she hadn't fallen in love with him, and if he hadn't convinced her that he loved her too.

After the night they'd kissed, Nick had continued to seek her out. And despite resolving every day not to have anything to do with him, she'd go with him, though walking or playing cards or even working out together had been pretty much as far as it had gone. Inevitably word had got around the camp about her and Nick.

One evening, as she was getting ready for bed, Sue had come to sit on the edge of her bed.

'Do you know what you're doing, Tiggy?' she asked.

The sun and dust was playing hell with her light skin. Tiggy finished rubbing moisturiser onto her neck before answering. 'What do you mean?'

'Come on, Tiggy. I've seen the way you look at each other. I've never seen him so bowled over by someone, but that's not to say it will last. Your tour will come to an

end soon, you'll be going home, and he'll be staying here.'
She took Tiggy's hand. 'I don't want you to get hurt. Nick
will move on to someone else. Maybe not straight away,
but eventually. That's the way he is.'

Tiggy gave up trying to pretend she didn't know what
Sue was talking about. Of course she'd wondered the same
thing.

She sat down next to her new friend. 'I can't help it. I
know I should stay away from him, but I can't. I love him,
Sue, and, as crazy as it sounds, I know I'll never stop.'

'Oh, Tiggy, I'm *not* saying he doesn't care about you.
How could he not? It's just that it never lasts with Nick. I
wish I could say it would be different with you...'

'Perhaps this time you'll be wrong.'

Sue looked at her for a long moment. She shook her
head. 'Perhaps you're right. I hope so, for your sake. He's
got to settle down some time, so why not with you? But
take care, Tiggy. Please.'

Sue's words stayed with Tiggy. Her friend was right.
Nick would tire of her sooner or later—it was inevitable.
If he was attracted to her now, it was because she hadn't
succumbed to him completely and because she wouldn't
be around for much longer. As soon as she left he would
move on to the next woman who intrigued him. So by the
time the following evening came around she'd decided to
finish it—whatever 'it' was. She sent a message saying
that she couldn't meet him at their usual place. She wasn't
really surprised when he came looking for her.

'What's up, Tiggy?' He stepped into her tent without
giving her a chance to reply. 'You okay?' He placed one
hand on her forehead and the other on her wrist. Typical
Nick to think the only reason she wasn't meeting him was
because she was ill. And she did feel ill. Not physically,

but ill at the thought that this would be the last time she felt his touch.

She jumped to her feet and moved away from him. It was so easy when she was away from him to tell herself that she could live without him, but now, with his presence filling her tent, his eyes warm with concern, she couldn't imagine a life without him.

She kept her back towards him, knowing that if she looked at him she'd be undone.

'It's over, Nick,' she said quietly.

His laugh was incredulous. 'Over?' He came to stand behind her and wrapped his arms around her waist. 'You're kidding, right?'

'I have never been more serious.'

He pulled her around until she was forced to face him. He lifted his thumb, tracing the curve of her mouth. She shivered and closed her eyes.

'I'm sorry, but I can't do this, Nick,' she whispered.

He frowned. 'Do what?'

'I can't be with you and pretend that it means nothing. I'll be going back home in a week but you'll be staying here.' She forced a smile. 'Don't even try to pretend that there won't be others after I've left.'

He dropped his hands and studied her for a long moment. 'What are you saying?'

'I'm saying that it's over. Time for us both to move on.'

'Hell, Tiggy. What do you want from me?'

What did she want from him? She sighed inwardly. Nothing much. Only his heart and soul, for him to care about her the way she cared about him, and not for a few days or weeks but forever. Nothing else would do. She loved him, but she didn't want the leftover bits of him. She wanted it all. She raised her chin and told him.

But if she'd expected him to look at her with horror and run for the hills she was mistaken. Instead, a slow smile crossed his face. 'Typical Tiggy. Always have to tell it like it is. I think that's why I've fallen in love with you.'

His smile disappeared and a look of bafflement crossed his face. 'Did I just say I loved you? Hell, Tiggy.' He grinned. 'I don't know what it is about you, but I can't get you out of my head. I love you, you idiot. I admit it's come as a bit of surprise to me too. But I love you. God knows why, as you're the prickliest, most infuriating woman I've ever known.'

'And you're easy?' Tiggy snapped back. 'Personally I have never met a more arrogant, over-confident man who thinks that he deserves nothing but worship, who thinks that the world revolves around him, who thinks that all women should fall at his feet. God knows why I let myself fall in love with you. I must be a bigger idiot than I thought.'

They stared at each other for a moment. Then suddenly she was in his arms.

Tiggy was back at the hospital at six. She paused in the doorway. Nick was at the table again, still playing cards. When he looked over at her, for a moment she thought she saw pleasure in his brown eyes and the hint of a smile on his full mouth, but almost immediately his expression hardened and she knew she'd been mistaken.

He threw his cards on the table and excused himself. She could tell that it took every ounce of willpower for him not to limp as he came towards her.

'I thought I told you not to come back,' he ground out through clenched teeth.

'And I told you I was coming back whether you wanted me to or not. You see, Nick, even if you were in a position to give me orders, which you aren't, I'm no better at obeying them than you are.'

When he eyed her speculatively for a long moment she could almost see the wheels turning in his head. 'In that case, if you're so determined to act the part of a wife, I want you to tell the harridan of a ward sister that I'm coming home with you.'

Home. One simple word could still tear a hole in her heart. It hadn't been a home since he'd left. She should have put the house on the market, but couldn't bear to, not even when she knew without a shadow of a doubt that Nick wouldn't be coming back.

But that was not to say she wanted Nick within a mile of the house she considered hers. He had to be kidding if he thought it was even a remote possibility. It was one thing seeing him in hospital, but to have him back in the home they'd once shared? No, she didn't think she could do that.

'There is no reason why I have to be here,' he continued. 'Even if I decide to go ahead with the operation, I don't have to be in hospital until the day before the procedure. In the meantime, they won't sign me out unless I have somewhere to go and someone...' he raised his eyebrow, '...and I quote, who is "willing and able to look after you and ensure that you won't do anything you shouldn't".'

So she'd been right about the flare of hope in his eyes she'd seen earlier, only it hadn't been for her.

'We are, as you keep reminding me, still married and the house is still in both our names.'

He was right. But he'd long ago given up the right to live there.

He lowered his voice. 'I don't intend to actually come home with you, of course, but I need you to say I am.'

'You want me to lie for you?' she asked, finding her voice at last.

'Don't make me beg, Tiggy. But if I don't get out of here, I won't be responsible for my actions. You know how I hate being cooped up.'

Tiggy's breath came out on a sigh. She had no doubt that Nick would abscond from the hospital if she didn't agree.

'Look, I'll go to a hotel and even promise to take it easy. Just tell them that you're taking me home.'

She didn't want him in their—her—home. She wanted him out of her life again. She wanted… Her head was beginning to throb. She didn't know what she wanted. Actually, come to think of it, she wanted to poke her finger in Nick's wound and twist. She wanted to hit him with her fists, she wanted to let him stew here in hospital where she hoped he'd be bloody miserable.

She sighed again.

'I'm not lying for you. If I tell them you're coming home with me, then that's what's going to happen.'

He paused and studied her through narrowed eyes.

'Isn't there the small matter of your partner? Won't he object?'

Partner? What was he on about? 'What on earth do you mean?'

'I saw you. With two little girls. You were taking them out of the car.'

'You were in London?' she asked incredulously.

'I came to see you. That's when I saw you with them.'

'You came to see me? Why?'

'I wanted to make sure you were okay. As soon as I saw that you were, I left. I didn't think the father of your children would appreciate a visit from your ex.'

'The father of my children?' Then it dawned on her. She couldn't help it, she had to laugh. If only Nick knew that apart from a few awful attempts at dating she'd remained on her own in the years since he'd left. 'Nick, the children you saw me with are my nieces—Charlie's twins. I have them to stay on a regular basis.'

'The children are your brother's?' Something flashed in his eyes before the old hooded expression she remembered so well was back. 'I assumed they were yours. I know you always wanted children.'

Yes, she had. But didn't the idiot know that she wanted *his* children and not just anyone's?

The first time she'd brought up the subject they'd been married for a year. They'd been lying, limbs entangled, in their bed in the warm afterglow of lovemaking. She'd had her head on his chest as he'd run his fingers through her hair. He had been due to go back to Afghanistan the next morning and the thought of being without him again had been tearing her apart.

'I'm thinking of stopping the Pill,' she'd said.

His hand had stilled.

'What's the rush?'

She wriggled around so she could see his face. 'No rush. I'm just thinking long term. It's better to be prepared for pregnancy. You know, stop the Pill six months in advance, start taking folic acid, that sort of thing.'

He tossed the blanket aside and got out of bed. Even after all these years she remembered exactly what she'd been thinking—actually, not so much thinking as feeling—a lethargic longing to have him back in bed beside her. She'd certainly had no inkling of what was to come.

'I don't want children.' His back was towards her.

'I don't mean right now.' Her laugh had sounded shaky even to her own ears.

He turned to her and smiled. 'Good.'

'But I do want them some time, Nick. I know we've

never spoken about it, but I always assumed you wanted them, too.'

He sank back onto the bed and wrapped her in his arms, burying his face in her hair. 'You're all I want, all I need, Tigs.'

She'd knelt and placed her hands on either side of his face. She could never get enough of looking at him. She could never get enough of him. That was part of the reason she wanted his child. Children would make them complete.

'And you're everything I ever wanted.' She smiled. 'And everything I didn't even know I wanted. But to have a baby...'

He'd kissed her and immediately she wanted him again.

'You haven't stopped taking the Pill, have you?' he whispered into her hair.

'Of course not!'

'Then wait until I get back from Afghanistan and we'll talk about it again. In the meantime, we only have a short time before I have to leave and I know how I want to spend it.'

And as he buried his face in her hair, the subject had been forgotten. If only she had realised then...

Nick was looking at her, waiting for her to say something.

'You can have the spare room. I'll have to clear the twins' stuff out and evict the cats. They won't be best pleased, but it won't be for long.'

'You have cats?'

'Two.'

'And no new man?'

'No,' she admitted, but couldn't resist adding, 'At least, not living with me.'

Once more something shifted in his eyes, but once again it was gone in an instant. 'I'll be out of your hair within a

week.' He gave her a quirky smile that sent shock waves
down her spine. 'Now that that's settled, could you tell the
nurses while I get dressed?'

CHAPTER SEVEN.

'IT'S CHANGED,' NICK said, looking around the sitting room.

'Hardly surprising in six years,' Tiggy responded dryly. 'I've redecorated. And without your stuff…' The sentence hung in the air. 'Why don't you sit down?' she added. God, this was going to be so much more difficult than she'd imagined. It felt weird treating Nick like a stranger in the home they'd once shared.

Tiggy frowned at his solitary small bag. Nick always travelled light but this was ridiculous. 'Where's the rest of your stuff?'

'In storage.'

'In storage? After six years?'

'Don't need much.'

'But you must be staying somewhere?'

'I have a rented flat near the hospital in Birmingham. I considered buying but…' He shrugged.

She wasn't really surprised. Part of the problem when they'd been married had been Nick's refusal to put down roots. His reluctance to have children only the first sign that he couldn't cope with domestic life—at least, not with her.

'I'll put your bag in the spare room then I'll make us something to eat. Chicken stir-fry okay?'

'Sure.' He got to his feet. 'Let me help.'

For a moment she felt a smile cross her lips. Nick had been hopeless in the kitchen, but that hadn't stopped him from coming up behind her whenever she'd been cooking and distracting her by nibbling her ear lobe… The images came thick and fast: her stirring a pot, Nick standing behind her, his hands on her hips as he nibbled her neck, her turning in his arms to return his kiss—whatever was cooking on the stove burning but neither of them caring. Nick lifting her onto the kitchen counter, sweeping away the makings of the dinner with his hand, hiking up her dress, his hands under her bottom, his thumbs on her inner thighs. No wonder so many of the meals she'd cooked had ended up uneaten.

Sex had never been the problem. Whenever Nick had come home on leave they'd rarely made it to the bed, at least not until much, much later. He had barely come through the front door before he'd been kicking it closed and pulling off her clothes, kissing her, pinning her against the wall, his lips hard and demanding, snaking a path from her mouth, down her breasts and across her abdomen.

She'd matched him step for step; her hands on his waist, unbuckling his belt with fingers that had shaken with the urgency of her need for him. She'd never thought she could be so wild when it came to sex, but with Nick it had been hard to be anything but.

Good God, was the kitchen always so warm? She shook her head in an attempt to clear it. With memories like that, how the hell was she going to get through the next few days?

Somehow.

She chased the last of the images away and lost the smile. She would *not* remember that. She had to remember why they'd broken up, the stuff that had torn them apart.

'No. Stay where you are. I'll manage.'

His mouth tightened. 'For God's sake, Tiggy, I'm not an invalid. I'm perfectly able to help.'

'I wasn't making a reference to your physical health, Nick, I was simply remembering how useless you were in the kitchen. Last time I checked, you could barely make toast. Unless that's changed?'

When he smiled lazily, her bones turned to liquid. 'Hey, if you remember, I can do a mean dissection on a chicken or a carrot.'

She bit her lip. The sooner Nick was out of her life the better.

In contrast to her fevered memories, dinner was an awkward, stilted affair; more like those at the end of their marriage than the beginning of it.

'Tell me about the operation they're proposing, Nick. From what Luke told me, you don't really have a choice.'

Nick leaned back in his chair, tipping it up on its rear legs just as he always had.

'I took some shrapnel two years ago. I was out on a rescue that didn't go according to plan.'

She noticed he didn't say what the rescue had involved and she knew better than to ask. Besides, Luke had already told her most of it.

'Luckily I was wearing my Kevlar jacket, but a piece of exploding shrapnel found its way into the base of my neck. I was knocked out but when they X-rayed my spine they decided it was too risky to operate.'

'And now?'

'It's moved. I always knew it was a risk. They think it's better out than in.'

'And you? What do you think? Surely having the operation is a no-brainer?'

'You would think, huh? Unfortunately, they're going to

have to cut away some tissue that's grown over the shrapnel and they can't be certain what will happen when they do. It's possible, even likely, that the bit that's left is lying close to the nerves emerging from the spine and they might sever them if they try to remove it.

'On the other hand, if they leave the shrapnel where it is, it might not get any worse—or at least not for years. Either way, I might have to leave the military.' His eyes were bleak. The army was everything to Nick. More than she could ever be.

Even though he'd hurt her more than she could bear, a part of her longed to reach out to him, to comfort him. Instead, she clasped her hands together tightly.

'Luke told me you saved his life.' It was all she could think of to say to change the subject.

Nick shook his head irritably. 'It was what we are all trained to do, Tiggy. Something you never seemed to understand.'

'Only because you stopped talking about it.'

Silence fell. Then he leaned forward and placed his elbows on the table. 'Anyway, enough about me. I want to know about you.'

'What do you want to know?'

'Are you happy?'

Tiggy started clearing their plates. Happy? Her life was full and she was reasonably content but there was still a deep, dark void that nothing could fill. 'Let's not go there, Nick.'

'You were better off without me,' he added so quietly that she'd almost not heard him.

She whirled around. 'Don't put the break-up on me. You left me long before you walked out that door.'

'Oh? If I remember correctly, it was you who left me.'

'Only because I didn't know what else to do to make you...' Tiggy struggled to get her breathing under control.

'Make me what?' he asked quietly.

'I came back the next morning but you'd gone. In the end you were the one who gave up on us.'

'It was for the best, Tiggy.'

'It wasn't for you to decide that on your own.' She took a deep breath and when she was sure she could speak calmly, she continued. 'What's the point in raking up the past? I actually do have a good life, Nick. I run the A and E department, I have friends, my family, my nieces—'

'Your cats.' He picked up Spike and rubbed his head. 'I can see you have a life. A good, safe life. Isn't that what you always wanted?'

No, it bloody well wasn't, and he knew that. She wanted to shout at him, to rage and throw the plate she was holding at him. But what was the point?

'Pudding?' she asked instead.

The next morning, Nick was up and at the table by the time Tiggy stumbled bleary-eyed into the kitchen.

'Coffee?' he asked, holding up the pot.

She nodded and took the chair opposite him, noticing that they'd both instinctively taken the same places at the table they'd done during their marriage. It could have been six years ago. Except that they had been two different people then. It was these small domestic details that threatened to undo her.

'No run this morning?' She could have bitten her lip the moment she'd said the words.

Amusement gleamed in his eyes. 'Not unless I want to give the neighbours some fun at the sight of a man with a limp jogging.'

'Sorry, Nick. Of course.'

'But I do intend to go for a walk.'

'Do you want me to come with you? Just in case?'

He raised a sardonic eyebrow. 'In case?'

'You know. In case you need help.'

His chair scraped back. 'How many times do I have to say I don't need mothering?'

Tiggy stiffened. He couldn't have chosen words that would have hurt her more.

The next time she had brought up the subject of babies, Nick's reaction was even more dismissive. 'I don't know if I'm cut out to be a father.'

'Of course you are. You're loving, kind…patient… You'd make a brilliant dad.'

They were in a restaurant, celebrating their anniversary and the fact that Nick was home again. For a whole three weeks this time.

Nick waited until the waiter had poured them some more wine, before leaning over the table and taking her hand. 'Can't you be happy with what we have, Tiggy?' he asked.

'I am. But a baby! Now, that would make everything perfect.'

He sat back in his chair, his eyes guarded. Tiggy had noticed that increasingly, when he returned from a tour, it took him days to get back to the teasing, happy-go-lucky man she'd married.

'I don't want a child of mine growing up without a father.'

His words chilled her to the bone. Lately Nick had been refusing to talk about what was happening in Afghanistan, saying he wanted to forget about it while he was on leave—a natural response perhaps. However, she knew from the news that the fighting was getting more intense and the knowledge filled her with dread.

'Like you did?' she asked quietly. Nick had told her not long after they'd met that his father had died when he had been ten. When she'd tried to probe deeper, he'd distracted her by kissing her until she hadn't been able to think straight. Since then she'd asked him many times about his family, but it had become clear it was one more topic to add to a growing list that was off limits.

'It's nothing to do with my childhood.'

'Then why? Talk to me, Nick. Please.' They both knew she wasn't just talking about his childhood. If only she could get him to open up to her, perhaps everything would be all right. 'Tell me what's going on in Afghanistan at the moment.'

His expression remained shuttered. 'There is nothing to say. Nothing I want to say. Believe me, you're better off not knowing.'

'Don't treat me like a child. I read the news, I watch TV. Part of me doesn't want to see it or hear about it, but I can't help it. You're out there so I need to know.'

He smiled sadly. 'I'm safe, Tiggy. I don't go out on patrol any more.'

She knew that. She also knew Nick had been told that he was too valuable to risk close to the fighting as his experience was of more value back at Camp Bastion. He'd tried to protest and argue that he was needed out on FOBs with his men. It had been the first argument he'd lost. Not even Nick had been able to defy orders on a permanent basis. After that, Tiggy had begun to notice he'd stopped talking to her about his life on the base.

'You'll be leaving the army soon and there isn't an A and E department in the country that wouldn't be glad to have someone of your expertise.' Nick had spent two three-

month stints at the Royal London passing on his knowledge of emergency medicine to the doctors there. It had
been the happiest time, for her, of their married life. Nick
however, had been impatient to rejoin his regiment. That
had hurt, even though she'd tried to understand his reasons.

'Surely we can have a baby when you're settled back
here?' she continued. The thought of their baby had made
her smile. 'He or she will be just like you...'

Nick frowned. 'Can we leave this conversation to another time?'

'When? We've been married for almost three years.
Can't we at least agree that they're part of our future?'
Despite the warmth of the restaurant, she felt chilled. 'Do
you even want children, Nick?'

He sighed and looked away into the distance. 'One day,
perhaps.' He fiddled with his glass, his eyes softening.
'Come on, Tigs, let's not argue. Not tonight.' He reached
across the table and ran his thumb up the inside of her arm.
Desire for him pooled in her belly. Even after three years
one look, one touch was all it took. They would talk about
having children again when he'd finished with Afghanistan. She smiled. 'What are we waiting for? Let's go home.'

While Nick tapped away on his laptop, she fed the cats,
cleared away the breakfast table, scrubbed the kitchen
floor and put on a load of laundry.

Her frantic activity couldn't keep him out of her head.
She should have let him rot in that hospital ward. What
had she been thinking? She'd just about got over him and
now she was letting him back into her life. Her nice, safe,
contented, albeit grey and boring life.

Life had been so exciting with Nick. But the excitement
had brought more pain than she'd ever thought possible.
Six years it had taken her to get over him. Six long years.

Yet he still set her nerve endings on fire.

She thumped the washing machine to make it go on—she really needed to get it fixed someday—and stomped up to her room.

She dressed in jeans and a long-sleeved T-shirt and pulled her recalcitrant curls into a ponytail.

Now she felt more able to deal with him. She'd been at a disadvantage earlier in her Snoopy pyjamas. At least now she looked more like the grown-up, mature, sensible woman she was. She added a touch of lipstick and some foundation just for good measure, before stomping her way back down the stairs.

He still made her feel like a teenager. Damn the man.

A short while after they'd had lunch Nick went out for his walk. Unable to settle down to her computer, Tiggy tackled some more housework, tightened the loose wire on the washing machine and cleaned the windows till they shone. When he wasn't back by early evening she began to worry. Perhaps something had happened to him. He might have had a seizure—it was perfectly possible for someone with his kind of injury. Or maybe he'd fallen?

The roast in the oven was in danger of drying out and her anxiety was increasing with every minute that ticked slowly by. To hell with this! She'd rather risk his wrath by going out to look for him than sit here and do nothing. She'd just turned off the cooker and was picking up her jacket when she heard a knock on the door.

Her heart pinged around her chest. Was this someone calling to tell her he'd collapsed and she needed to come to the hospital straight away?

But when she opened the door it was to find Nick, holding a bunch of flowers, with a sheepish grin on his face.

'No key,' he said. 'Bought some flowers to say sorry. I

remembered tulips were your favourite. Took me a while to track them down.'

His smile melted her insides. That had always been the problem; she could never stay mad at him for long. But what was she thinking? He was a no-good, cold, self-centred man who had broken her heart and not even cared.

She grabbed the flowers from him and stepped aside to let him in. As he brushed past her she smelled alcohol on his breath.

'You've been drinking!' She was shocked. Nick never drank.

'So I have.' He grinned at her. 'Feels pretty good.'

'Are you out of your mind?'

He looked at her from the corners of his eyes. 'Perhaps.'

He took a few steps, his limp more evident than ever, before sinking into one of the armchairs.

Tiggy shoved the flowers into a vase and turned to face him. 'Do you really think that, given your current medical condition, it's wise to be drinking?'

'I'm pretty sure it's not wise. But when did I ever follow the path of reason?'

When indeed? 'I think you should go and lie down,' she said frostily.

He grinned again. This time it was nothing short of a leer. 'Great idea.' He struggled to his feet and swayed. Tiggy reached him before he fell. He threw his arm across her shoulder as she struggled to hold him up. Nick was over six feet tall and well built.

'You coming?' he asked. Then without warning he sank back onto the chair, pulling her with him. Somehow, she wasn't quite sure how, she landed on his lap.

She practically inhaled him as his arms tightened around her.

'God, you're still so beautiful,' he said roughly. 'Do you know how long it's been?'

For a split second she was tempted to stay where she was. It felt so good, so right to be back in his arms.

Thankfully she came to her senses. She pushed away from him and leaped to her feet. 'If it's sex you're wanting, Nick, I'm sure there's plenty out there who'll be happy to oblige. Any more of this and I'm taking you back to the hospital.'

'You wouldn't deny a dying man his last wish?' He reached out for her again but she avoided his grip.

Hands on hips, she raged at him. 'Of all the idiotic things to say. You think I feel sorry for you? Let me tell you, I've never felt less sorry for anyone in my life.'

Still blazing, she picked up a blanket from the back of the couch and flung it at him.

'Go to sleep, Nick. I'll see you in the morning.' And without giving him a chance to reply she flicked the sitting-room lights out and marched off to bed.

CHAPTER EIGHT

IT WAS A very sorry-looking Nick that she found in the kitchen the next morning, slumped over the table with his head in his hands, an empty pot of coffee in front of him.

'God, I know now why I never drink.'

Barely glancing in his direction, Tiggy opened the blinds. Sunshine streamed in.

Nick opened one eye then quickly closed it again. 'Do you have to shine a torch in my eyes? Do you have no pity?'

'Not much, no.' She put on a fresh pot of coffee and sat down at the other side of the table.

'How much did you have?'

'No idea. I stopped counting after the third—or was it the fourth?—pint.'

She went to the fridge, poured a glass of orange juice and shook some painkillers into her hand. She plonked them down on the table.

Nick winced. 'Could you do that a little more gently?'

He swallowed the tablets down with the orange juice then opened both eyes. 'I didn't behave very well, huh?'

'You behaved like an idiot, but I guess a *dying man* is allowed some leeway.'

He winced again. 'I did say that, didn't I?' He groaned.

'Can we forget about last night? I'm guessing, since I woke up on the chair, that my words didn't win a place in your bed.'

Tiggy had to laugh. 'It wasn't one of your best chat-up lines, Nick, no.'

'What was my best, Tiggy? Do you remember?'

'Unfortunately I remember too much—the good the bad and the plain hurtful.'

Nick studied her for a long moment through dark, sombre eyes then raked a hand through his hair. 'This was a bad idea. I'll check into a hotel,' he said quietly.

Regardless of how difficult it was having him there, she couldn't turn him out. Surely they could manage a couple of days together? She swallowed. 'There's no need for you to do that. We—our marriage—are all in the past. You can stay here…as long as you promise me, no more drinking.'

His mouth tipped up at the corners and the darkness left his eyes. 'I promise. Now, how about I attempt to make us some scrambled eggs?'

The rest of the day passed as if they were an old married couple. Nick read the papers while Tiggy caught up on a report she had to do for work. Often she'd catch him looking at her with a puzzled expression.

Later that night, unwilling to break the harmony but knowing she had to, she waited until after dinner to raise the subject of his operation.

'Have you decided what to do?' she asked.

He glanced up from his laptop. 'About what?'

'The operation, of course.'

'Oh, that. Yes.'

'And I don't suppose you're going to share with me what that decision is?'

'I'm going to have it, of course. It's the only logical decision. If I do nothing, the shrapnel will keep moving. At least with the operation I won't have the sword of Damocles hanging over my head forever.'

How could he sound so calm, as if it was a stranger they were talking about? But then, that was Nick—the Nick of their last year of marriage. Closed off, unwilling to discuss anything, not even when it was clear to both of them that their marriage had been crumbling. Although she'd tried desperately to find him again, to keep their love alive, she hadn't been able to reach him.

After their anniversary dinner, everything had seemed to get worse. Whenever he'd been home on leave he'd prowl around the house like a caged tiger or go for runs without her that had lasted for hours. Then he'd started going away on his own for days at a time. Mountain climbing— or so he'd said.

She'd tried everything. Invited friends around for dinner, stopped inviting friends around for dinner, booked them romantic weekends away in the country, arranged walks, parties—everything she could think of to make life exciting for him, hoping that he'd forget about Afghanistan.

None of it worked. If anything, whatever she did seemed to push him further away. In the end she stopped trying to reach him, hoping that when he left the army the old Nick would return and everything would be as it had been in the beginning.

Then, as he became increasingly tense and withdrawn, she began to wonder if Nick was having an affair. It would explain his silence, his lack of engagement with her when he was at home. It would also go some way to explain why he kept putting off the decision to have a child.

But she couldn't believe that Nick would do that to her. He was impatient, difficult, but deceitful? No. She would have staked her life on his loyalty. Did he still love her? Sometimes she was certain of it. Other times, when he was in Afghanistan and she so alone in their bed that seemed far too big without him, she wondered if he was only staying with her because he believed it was the right thing to do.

They still made love. Their incessant need for each other had never disappeared, but she knew that somewhere in the darkest part of his mind he was lost to her.

She would never hold on to him if he didn't love her anymore. She would rather lose him than have him stay for all the wrong reasons—even if the thought of losing him felt like having her heart ripped from her body. She couldn't go on living with him not knowing if he still cared. She couldn't go on living with him and not knowing.

She met him at the airport and he lifted her and hugged her so tightly he almost squeezed the breath from her body.

'God, it's so good to see you,' he whispered into her hair. 'Sometimes the thought of being without you…'

He didn't finish the sentence and on the drive back home he was preoccupied, only half listening to her chatter on.

But she'd become accustomed to that and she still hoped she was wrong about everything. Perhaps when he was out of the army for good, the Nick she'd known would come back to her. Perhaps the best thing to do was wait?

One thing that hadn't changed was their need for each other. With the dark winter nights closing in, Nick lit a fire after they'd made love and they lay together, still naked, wrapped in each other's arms, watching the flames cast shadows on the ceiling.

'How was this tour?' she asked eventually.

'Same as always.'

She sat up and hugged her knees to her chest. 'Come on, Nick, you can do better than that.'

He placed his hands behind his head. 'It was grim. Is that what you want to hear? We lost two boys and sent another half-dozen home without limbs.'

Tiggy sucked in a breath. 'I heard some of it on the news. I'm so sorry. But what about the ones you saved?'

'It's not enough just to save them.'

'You're not God, Nick. You can't let every case tear you apart. Thank goodness you'll be out of it soon.'

He looked away. 'There's something I need to tell you. I've signed on for another tour.'

Tiggy stared at him in disbelief. 'You what?'

'I know I said I wasn't going to, Tigs, and I promise after the time's up I'll leave. I'll do anything, go anywhere. We can even have the family you want.'

'The family I want? You talk as if having a family is a favour to me—some sort of compensation. That you agreeing to have a child is going to make it all right that you signed up again when we agreed you wouldn't.'

'Tiggy...' He reached for her but she jumped up and out of his reach. In the past she'd always let their lovemaking heal the wounds between them. But no more. Couldn't he see what was happening to their marriage?

'The men need me,' he said softly.

'Please don't try and make me feel guilty for wanting my husband back. Because you've been gone for a long time, Nick. And not just when you've been in Afghanistan. I need you, Nick. What about me? I'm your wife. I don't even know why you married me.'

'I married you because I love you. I never thought it would be this hard.'

'Life with me is hard? Oh, Nick.' Her chest was tight. Feeling dead inside, she walked upstairs, quickly got dressed and threw some clothes into an overnight case. When she came back downstairs Nick was staring into the fire. He didn't even seem to notice that she was holding a bag.

'I'm going to my mother's,' she said. 'While I'm gone I want you to think about what you want. Me or the army. It's your choice.' She couldn't even cry. If he'd taken her in his arms then, if he'd done anything to convince her otherwise, she would have stayed. But when he made no move, he gave her no choice.

'Goodbye, Nick,' she said. Then she stepped out into the cold night air.

And until the day at the hospital she hadn't seen him again.

Nick was looking at her. She realised she hadn't replied. 'I think you're making the right decision,' she said.

'Good.' He turned back to his computer screen.

Are you frightened? she wanted to ask. She almost laughed out loud. Nick frightened? Not in this lifetime. No, the only thing that scared him was commitment and the thought of being tied down.

He glanced over at her. 'If I don't make it, as you're still my wife, you'll get everything.'

Good God—as if she cared a jot about that! What did he take her for? 'I don't need anything from you. I can manage fine. I've managed perfectly well on my own for the last six years.'

He narrowed his eyes. 'When you wouldn't take maintenance, I put it all in a deposit account. It's there when you need it.'

Tiggy gritted her teeth.

'I have no intention of taking your money, Nick. And you are going to be fine. I won't, I repeat won't, have this conversation again. Now, if you'll excuse me, I'm going to bed.'

* * *

The next morning, Nick made himself coffee, feeling worse than he'd done the previous day. What the hell was he doing here? He'd barely slept at all. He kept seeing the pain in Tiggy's eyes when they'd talked last night. Was it possible she still cared? In that case, to come here, to the home they'd once shared, had been madness.

Even after all these years she still did something to his insides no woman before or since had.

Why hadn't she signed the divorce papers? She deserved to find happiness with someone else instead of an emotionally bankrupt, potentially soon to be ex-army doctor, who couldn't give her what she wanted.

Permanence. A family. A future.

He should never have married her, but he hadn't been able to help himself. He'd fallen for her before he'd known what was happening and had allowed himself to believe that she could save his soul and fill the emptiness inside him.

It was only later that he'd realised he didn't have a soul to save.

Where was she anyway? In their too-short married life, she'd always been up early, accompanying him on his runs. He smiled at the memory. Over the years she'd taken up running with a vengeance until she'd almost been able to keep up with him. Her determination was one of things he'd loved most about her—that and her soft heart.

One of the cats jumped into his lap and lay there purring, stretching its paws in ecstasy. Nick had never expected to find Tiggy still living in their home, surrounded by cats instead of babies.

The door swung open and he heard her deep breathing before he saw her. When she came into the kitchen his heart kicked. God, she looked good in a cropped top that exposed her flat stomach and tiny shorts that emphasised her long, slender legs.

She glanced at him coolly. 'Coffee on the go?'

'Can I pour you some?'

She shook her head, opening the fridge and taking out some orange juice. She held it towards him with a raise of one eyebrow and when he shook his head she poured some into a tall glass.

'You still run, then?' he asked. 'Hell, that was a stupid question.'

A small smile tugged at her lips before quickly disappearing. 'I'd hardly mow the lawn dressed like this.' She turned her cool blue eyes on the cat. 'He bothering you?'

'No. He's fine. I never thought of you as a cat lover.'

'Seems there was quite a bit we didn't know about one another,' she said shortly. Then she sighed and sat down at the table. 'Sorry. I promised myself I wasn't going to bitch about the past.'

'I wouldn't blame you if you did.' Silence hung between them. Nick shifted in his chair. 'You never met anyone else?' He had to know.

Something flashed in her eyes before she regarded him steadily. 'Now, why would you think that?' Her smile was tight. 'What did you think, Nick? That I sit at home night after night with only my cats for company, content to let life pass me by?'

It didn't matter that he'd told himself over the years that she would meet someone else and it would be for the best. The thought of her in someone else's arms turned his stomach.

She studied him over the rim of her glass. 'As a matter of fact, I am going out tonight. I'm sure you'll cope on your own for a few hours.'

Jealousy wound like a snake in his guts. 'Of course.' What else could he say? Even if he wanted to bar the door.

She finished her juice and got up from the table. 'Now, if you'll excuse me, I have things to do. She waved vaguely in the direction of the kitchen. 'You know where to find everything.'

As she stalked out without a backward glance, Nick knew for certain that even if she'd stopped loving him, his feelings for her were far from dead. He groaned. He should never have come here, but he'd been unable to stop himself from stealing this bit of time with her. He was a selfish bastard. If he had been no good for her back then, he was less so now.

Now, why had she lied about going out? Just because Nick had implied that she didn't have a life was no reason to make up a date that didn't exist. Over the last few years friends had always been trying to set her up with someone. But no matter how much she told herself that the banker or teacher or whoever it was she faced across a dining-room table was perfectly nice, good looking and decent company, they never matched up to Nick. Not for a single second.

In the end she'd put her foot down with her friends. No more dates, she'd told them. She would rather, in fact, chew off her arm than waste another moment of her life listening to someone in whom, when all was said and done, she wasn't remotely interested.

None of that helped with tonight's predicament. Sally was out of town, Lucy just had another baby and it was too short notice to call any of her other friends. Besides, what would they say when they learned that Nick was staying with her?

They'd tell her she was out of her mind—and they'd be right.

She showered and tried to settle down at her desk to work. She hadn't been lying when she'd said she had work to do. But, acutely aware of Nick's footsteps and the occasional opening and closing of a door, she couldn't concentrate.

Once he popped his head round her door and asked if she wanted anything from the shop as he was going to stretch his legs.

'You might want to get something for your evening meal,' she said. 'Remember I'm going out.'

'For dinner?' he asked with a lift of his brow.

'Yes. Not that it's any business of yours but I have a date.'

She thought she saw something flash in his eyes but almost immediately he resumed his deadpan expression. 'Good for you,' he said.

Crap.

That evening, she dressed as if she were really going on a date. She chose a jade silk dress she'd decided was too short once she'd tried it on again at home but had never got around to returning, and scrunched her hair into ringlets, letting it fall free down her back. She left her legs bare and slipped on a pair of high heels.

She applied more make-up than usual—a dark metallic shadow the beautician in the high-street store had promised would bring out the colour of her eyes and a red lipstick that somehow, instead of clashing with her hair, gave her confidence.

While she was getting ready she wondered where she could actually go. She'd have to be away for at least three hours to make a date seem convincing. She tried not to think about why she was going ahead with a charade that was childish as well as pointless.

One thing she did know was that she couldn't back out now. Either she'd have to admit to making up the date or she'd have to pretend a last-minute cancellation. Neither option appealed to her. The first because she didn't want Nick questioning her reasons for fibbing, the second because she didn't want to him think, even for a moment, that her imaginary date had cancelled. The humiliation of Nick thinking she'd been stood up was too much to even contemplate.

She almost changed her mind at that point. What did it matter what he thought? He wasn't part of her life any more. He would have the operation, recover and be on his way. She would never see him again.

So why didn't the knowledge cheer her up?

She added mascara for good measure and clipped on a diamond and jade bracelet. If she was going to do a Mata Hari she may as well go the whole hog.

Taking a deep breath and plastering an expectant smile on her face, she sashayed downstairs.

But to her chagrin, when she reached the sitting room, it was to find Nick fast asleep on the sofa.

She stood over him. Even in the semi-darkness she could see he was frowning in his sleep. What demons tormented him?

Her heart stumbled. What had happened to the Nick she'd fallen in love with? Where had the irrepressible, fun-loving man disappeared to?

A lock of hair had fallen over his brow. That too was different. In the past he'd always worn his hair cropped short. Unable to resist the urge, she bent over him and gently smoothed the errant lock of hair from his face.

His eyes snapped open and his hand wrapped around her wrist like a spring. The coldness in his gaze shocked her.

'What the hell?' he said. Still holding her wrist, he sat up. 'Don't you know better than to sneak up on a man when he's asleep?'

'Come on, Nick,' she said, trying to pull her hand away. But he held it in his vice-like grip. 'Don't you think you're overreacting?'

'You wouldn't say that if you spent nights sleeping with your weapon next to you, waiting for the next attack, not knowing when it would come or what you were going to have to deal with when it did.'

'I'm sorry,' she said softly. 'I didn't think.'

He sighed and finally let her hand go. It was painful where he'd grabbed her and she rubbed it absentmindedly.

His eyes softened. 'Did I hurt you? Let me see.'

He took her hand more gently this time and turned it over. Red marks, almost as if she'd been handcuffed, had appeared.

'It's okay,' she said. 'Really.' The touch of his fingertips burned her skin worse than his grip had and her heart started to pound.

The pad of his thumb ran circles over the inside of her arm and her pulse upped another notch. He was bound to feel it racing. She snatched her hand away again and hid it behind her back.

She sat down on the sofa next to him.

'Tell me,' she said. 'Tell me what it was like. Help me to understand.'

He laughed harshly. 'Some things are better not spoken about.'

And that, of course, had been the problem. He'd refused to talk about it when they had still been together, even when he'd cried out in his sleep and she'd woken to find him entangled in their sheets and covered in sweat. If he wouldn't speak to her then, what made her think he'd talk to her now?

'Anyway,' he said, 'I thought you had a date.'

Oops. She'd forgotten.

His eyes travelled over her. He whistled. 'Lucky man. But don't you think that dress is a little short?'

She stood, all the old exasperation returning. 'No. And may I remind you, Nick, you're not my father.'

'As if I need any reminding.'

She tucked her hair behind her ears and picked up her bag. 'I have my mobile phone if you need me.' As soon as the words were out of her mouth she could have bitten her lip. If Nick noticed the irony he said nothing.

'Unlikely,' he said shortly. 'I'm going to watch football and make myself a sandwich. After that I'll probably go to bed.'

Tiggy swallowed her disappointment. Couldn't he even look marginally put out that she was going on a date with another man?

And *apparent* was the key word, she reminded herself. She still hadn't decided how she was going to kill enough time to prevent him thinking she'd been dumped. The library? No, that closed at eight. A coffee shop or restaurant? No, that was too sad. A movie, then. It was all that was left.

She smiled as coolly as she could and walked out the door.

In the cinema she couldn't focus on the film. All she could think about was Nick. Why had he come back into her life now? And like this? It was torture sharing the house with him again.

But surely she could cope with a few more days? She

would be at work during the day, and could perhaps find an excuse to go out in the evening.

No. She was being ridiculous. It wasn't as if she could pretend to have a date every night. And besides, after six years surely she could manage to be around Nick for a little longer? She'd be polite, distant, cool. He would never know how much he'd hurt her.

She took another handful of tasteless popcorn and chewed morosely. The couple on the screen were kissing, her hands snaking around his neck, him kissing her as if he wanted to devour her... Tiggy knew only too well how that had felt. Couldn't she have found a different film? Something with no love scenes, for example? But, then, didn't every film have at least a small love story?

She glanced around. Everyone was with someone, except her. Most couples were holding hands as they stared at the screen; some were with children.

Families. She sighed again. Wherever she went, she was surrounded by children. This hadn't been one of her better ideas.

Her thoughts returned relentlessly to Nick. What if the operation went wrong? What if he was left paralysed, brain damaged—or worse? For someone as vital, as physically and mentally active as Nick, death would be preferable. She reached into her bag for her mobile, surreptitiously switching it on. What if he'd become unwell? What if he'd had a seizure and was lying on the floor, calling for help?

What if he was dead?

Of course he wasn't. If his life were in any immediate danger they would never have let him leave the hospital. But then again he'd forced the issue and they'd only reluctantly agreed because Luke had told them she was an A and E nurse.

She could call him. One little phone call to see if he was

okay. If he answered she could hang up without speaking, but at least she'd know he was fine.

She crept along the row of cinema-goers, whispering her apologies as she went and slipped out into the foyer.

One phone call. He'd answer and then she could go back to her film. That would seem perfectly reasonable. Of course she wouldn't hang up—that would be childish and cowardly. Anyway, he'd probably phone the number back and then she'd have to explain herself.

She closed her eyes and sighed. Why was she behaving like a schoolgirl anyway? All this pretending to be out on a date so that her ex-husband, her *very* ex-husband, wouldn't realise that there was no one in her life was ridiculous.

Not that she was going to admit the truth. That would be too humiliating. He didn't have to know she'd never so much as had a second date with a man since they'd separated, never mind another relationship. So when Nick answered the phone she would simply say she was checking on him while her companion was in the bathroom. That was perfectly reasonable, *mature* behaviour.

When he didn't answer her landline she tapped in the number of his mobile. She let it ring until it went to voicemail, thought of leaving a message and decided against it.

A few minutes later she tried again. No reply. She tried another four times, waiting for several minutes between each call, her anxiety rising by the second.

Why wasn't he answering?

Her head filled with images of Nick lying helpless on the floor and she made up her mind. What had she been thinking? What was this whole fiasco about? Even if Nick was perfectly well and watching his game, not even noticing, never mind caring that she wasn't there, he could be dead in a few days and she was sitting in a half-empty cinema because of her pride?

She rushed outside, jumping impatiently from foot to foot as taxi after taxi sailed past.

Eventually she managed to hail one, squirming with frustration every time they stopped at a red light.

Finally she was home. She shoved some money into the driver's hand. Her own hands were trembling so badly she dropped her keys before she was finally able to get the right one into the lock and let herself inside.

The house was in darkness. God, oh, God, she was right. He was lying somewhere, unconscious and unable to call for help. Her heart in her mouth, she opened the door of her sitting room.

Nick was sitting on the sofa, his long legs propped up on the stool in front of him, a beer in one hand, watching rugby. He must have showered in the time she'd been away as his hair was damp and he was shirtless. She averted her eyes from the sight of his muscled chest.

He glanced her way in mild surprise and immediately returned his attention to the TV screen.

'Have a good time?' he asked mildly.

So he'd noticed she'd gone—even if he hadn't noticed she was back remarkably early for someone who was supposed to be on a dinner date.

All of a sudden, for some reason, the sight of him infuriated her. It was hard to believe that only minutes before she'd been imagining his death with a bleeding heart.

She stalked over and removed the beer from his hand. 'I thought we agreed that this isn't good for you.'

'It's non-alcoholic beer.' He smiled, reaching for it. 'When did you get so bossy? I don't remember bossy.' His eyes glinted. 'I remember assertive—particularly when it came to sex—but not bossy.'

Her breath caught in her throat.

'That was then,' she retorted. 'A long, long time ago.'

He switched off the TV. He'd lost some weight, she thought distractedly, his jeans were lying low on his hips. Her eyes followed the dark hair that started just below his navel and finished… She shook her head. Don't go there.

He glanced at his watch and frowned. 'Aren't you home a bit early for someone on a date? Did he stand you up?'

'Of course not!' It wasn't a lie. If someone didn't exist, he couldn't stand anyone up. But maybe next time she could borrow a real-life man, perhaps Lucy's husband. God, she was off in her fantasy world again. 'I'm home early because I was worried about you. Didn't you hear the phone ring? Why didn't you answer?'

'I didn't think I should answer your landline.'

Tiggy gritted her teeth. 'I also called your mobile. Several times.'

'You called me? In the middle of a date?' He felt in his pockets and shrugged. 'Must have left it in my room.'

She felt like such an idiot. His eyes creased at the corners as realisation dawned. 'You abandoned your date? Because you were worried about me?'

'You're my responsibility,' she replied. 'I shouldn't have left you alone.'

He narrowed his eyes. 'I am not your—or anyone else's—responsibility.' He sprang to his feet so that he was towering over her. 'I never have been and never will be. A piece of shrapnel doesn't make me anyone's responsibility.' He glared down at her before turning on his heel. He stalked out of the room, returning seconds later with his phone. 'You called me eight times? Good God, Tiggy, your date must have the patience of a saint.'

His mouth turned up at the corners and his eyes glinted. 'Did you tell him it was your husband you were phoning?

Did you tell him that your husband was staying with you? In the home we once shared?'

That was the trouble with lies—once you started with them you wrapped yourself up in them like a ball of string.

She shrugged, trying to look casual. 'He's a grown man. He knows it's been over for years.'

Something flickered across his face. Disbelief. Possessiveness? Amusement? She couldn't tell. All she knew was that her heart was racing. Suddenly his eyes softened. 'I'm glad you're back,' he said. He picked up a lock of her hair and twirled it in his fingers. 'I missed you.'

Now her heart was galloping like a runaway horse. Was he talking about just now? Or the last six years? Her body swayed towards him as if it had a mind of its own and before she knew what she was doing she'd raised her face, wanting, needing to feel his mouth on hers.

But to her mortification he turned away.

'Go to bed, Tiggy,' he said harshly, 'before I do something we'll both regret.'

CHAPTER NINE

THE NEXT DAY Tiggy used her lunch-break to go up to the children's ward. Jo Green had been admitted to A and E two weeks earlier with meningococcal sepsis. Sadly her parents hadn't recognised how ill their daughter was until the rash had appeared on Jo's arms and legs. By the time the ambulance had brought her in, she had been unconscious and had needed to be put on life support. The medical team had done everything they could, pushing IV antibiotics and fluids, and the girl had survived.

However, two days later her legs had developed gangrene and Jo had had to have both her legs amputated above the knee. Tiggy had popped up to see her and the parents several times before. In A and E, when you held a child's life in your hands, strong bonds often developed between the nurses and the parents. She and the Greens had been no different.

Mr and Mrs Green were, as usual, by their daughter's bedside. Jo was staring up at the ceiling, just as she'd done ever since she'd discovered her legs had been amputated.

'How are you today, Jo?' Tiggy asked softly.

Jo's eyes flicked towards Tiggy. 'I want them to go.'

'Who?'

'Those two. The ones who call themselves my parents but who let this happen to me.'

Jo's mother, Colleen, winced. 'Darling, we had no choice.' Her face was pale. It was clear she hadn't been sleeping. 'Don't you think I would have given my life to save yours?'

'Whatever.'

'Now, Jo,' her father said. He appeared to be in no better condition than his wife. 'Your mum is telling the truth.'

Colleen looked at Tiggy with anguished eyes. 'If only we'd taken her to the doctor sooner.'

'Yes,' Jo snarled. 'And if only you hadn't told them they could take my legs.'

'Sweetheart, we had no choice. You would have died if we hadn't agreed to the operation.'

'I'd be better off dead,' Jo said flatly. 'What sort of life do you think I'm going to have now? Who in their right mind is going to want to go out with a girl who doesn't have any legs? Who is going to want to be with someone who is no use to anyone? Who can't even go to the bathroom without help?'

'Can't you talk to her?' Colleen whispered to Tiggy.

Tiggy sat down on the bed. 'I know it's horrible now, but I promise you, you will have a life. In time you'll learn to walk again. You'll be able to do most of the things if not all the things you could do before.'

'Walk on wooden legs? You have to be kidding me.'

'They won't be wooden, darling. Remember that nice lady came up to show you what they'd be like?' Colleen pleaded.

'Oh, Mum. You're such a…' Jo bit down on her lip and blinked furiously.

Tiggy squeezed the teenager's hand. 'I'll come and see you tomorrow,' she said.

'Don't bother. What could you—what can any of you—know what it's like to be me? You have no idea.'

Colleen walked Tiggy to the door. 'What are we going to do? She just lies there. The physios can't do anything with her except some passive exercises. They say she needs to get out of bed and moving, but she won't even try to sit up. She won't eat. It's as if she hates us.'

'It's natural for her to feel angry and blame you,' Tiggy said, 'but give her time.'

'She was a runner, you know. Up for selection for the national training squad for the next Olympics. It was her life.'

'The same strength that made her a possibility for the squad will stand her in good stead when she's ready to accept what's happened to her.'

'And I'm afraid that that same strength of character will keep her from accepting what's happened. I know my daughter, Tiggy. Nothing you or I could say will make a difference. Unless she believes that she has a life worth living, I just don't know what she'll do.'

When Tiggy got home that evening she was still thinking about Jo.

Nick was in the kitchen, studying a recipe book and glancing at a chicken as if it was about to leap off the kitchen counter and attack him. He was wielding a knife like it was a scalpel.

'I thought I would make dinner,' he said, 'but I'm having a bit of a problem. How the hell do I make chicken stock?' But then he must have seen her face as he laid the knife on the counter and pulled out a chair for her.

'Sit down.'

She opened her mouth to speak but he shook his head. He reached into the fridge and poured a glass of wine and waited until she'd taken a sip. 'Now, tell me what's wrong?'

'How do you know something's wrong?'

'Because I've seen that shell-shocked look on nurses' and medics' faces too often not to recognise it. Did something happen at work? Did you have a bad case?'

It was a relief to have someone to talk to who knew what it was like. 'She came to us last week, Jo, I mean. She's fifteen, waiting for her GCSE results, a world-class runner, one of life's gifted and blessed children. At least, she was.'

Nick said nothing, just waited quietly for her to continue.

'She was diagnosed with bacterial meningitis. We didn't need to have the results of her lumbar puncture to know. It was evident from the rash straight away. Her parents thought she had flu and was feeling particularly bad because she'd been training so much. Anyway, by the time they recognised that she was seriously ill and called an ambulance Jo was already beginning to drift away. She lost consciousness on the way to hospital. We did everything we could. The works. But as you know, at that stage it was just a fight to save her life. And we did.

'She was transferred to ITU and I went up most days to see her. I was the nurse who liaised with the family. You know what it's like. They turn to you as if you are the only thing between them and this awful chasm. It's like a battle and you and they have joined forces.'

'I know,' Nick said.

'Anyway, two days after she was admitted to ITU she developed gangrene. There was nothing anyone could do except amputate. Both legs. Above the knee. She's only fifteen.'

Nick came to stand behind her and squeezed her shoulders. She let her head fall back against him.

'There's so much they can do now,' he said softly. 'They've—we've—had so much experience with amputees.'

'She's just a teenager, Nick. She thinks her life is over. She won't even get out of bed let alone start her proper physio. Her parents are beside themselves. They don't know how to get through to her. No one knows how to get through to her.'

Nick was quiet for so long she started to wonder if in his head he'd gone back to Afghanistan. Suddenly she was horrified. Of course talking about Jo must bring back memories for him.

'I think I know what we can do.' He leaned over her and picked up his mobile from the kitchen table. 'Leave this to me,' he said. Suddenly he smiled. 'In the meantime, could you see what you can do with that bloody chicken?'

He wouldn't say what he was up to, but the next morning he insisted on coming with her to the hospital. He was looking particularly pleased with himself. In fact, he was looking more relaxed than she had seen him since they'd met again.

This Nick reminded her of the one she'd fallen in love with.

Oops, she told herself. Don't go there. One swallow does not a summer make.

'If you have some bright idea about marching up to see Jo and telling her to pull herself together as there are many people in worse positions, forget it.'

He slid his eyes in her direction. 'Do you think I'm that insensitive—or clueless?'

'Then tell me what you're up to.'

'Nope, no can do. You'll have to wait.' He reached over and tweaked her nose. 'You always were a curious woman.'

'Did you just tweak my nose?' she spluttered.

He just laughed. 'God, I've missed you.'

She didn't know what to say to that so she didn't say

anything. But she couldn't stop the warm glow that spread from her toes right up to the middle of her chest.

She shook her head. No. Definitely no. No way. Not in a million years. As soon as it was decent she was kicking him out of her house and back out of her life.

When Tiggy pulled into the car park, Nick almost leaped out of the car. His eyes searched until they came to rest on a beautiful blonde standing by the entrance. When his face broke into a wide smile, an unpleasant sensation gathered in the pit of Tiggy's stomach. Not jealousy—of course not—only an unpleasant feeling.

The woman smiled back and raised her hand. She came running over to them and flung her arms around Nick's neck.

Tiggy wanted to slap her. And Nick.

'Hey, Hazel, it's good to see you.'

'You too, boss. It's been far too long.'

'Hazel, this is Tiggy. Tiggy, Corporal Hazel Gray—one of the best army medics I ever had the pleasure of working with.'

None of that made Tiggy want to slap her any less. However, she made herself smile as she held out her hand. She was still puzzled. Why was Nick meeting her here?

'How's that husband of yours?' Nick said as he hooked Hazel's elbow in his and started to walk towards the main entrance.

She had a husband! Tiggy's breath came out in a whoosh; she hadn't realised she'd been holding it. They were walking ahead of her and Hazel was saying something to Nick that made him laugh. The jealousy she felt this time was different. They were so easy with one another, easy in a way she couldn't remember ever being with

Nick. Life with him had been exciting, fun—at least at first—but easy? No. Not that. Especially towards the end.

Feeling a little like an unwelcome guest at a party, she followed them. Hazel was tall and slim, but there was something in the way she walked that wasn't quite right. She was rolling slightly as she walked. It was almost indiscernible and if Tiggy hadn't been behind them she would never have noticed.

'Which way to Jo's ward?' Nick asked once they were inside the hospital.

'I think you should tell me what's going on.'

Hazel frowned. 'You mean you haven't told her?'

'No. I wanted to see if she noticed. And you didn't, did you, Tiggy?'

Tiggy was beginning to see where this was going. But it wasn't something she felt comfortable about asking.

'Hazel is a double amputee,' Nick said.

If they hadn't told her, Tiggy wouldn't have believed it.

Hazel's eyes dimmed, but just for a moment. 'I was the medic with the boys when the man in front of me stood on an IED. He didn't make it, and I was in a bad way. Nick was part of the rapid response team. He kept me alive.' Nick gave a dismissive shake of his head. 'You know you did,' Hazel said with a soft smile. 'Anyway, he told me about the girl with the double amputations. He thought it would be a good idea for me to speak to her. I do a lot of that now I'm no longer in the army.'

They stopped walking as Hazel continued.

'When I lost my legs, I thought my life was over. I hated Nick for saving me. My husband Davie and I were engaged at the time, but I didn't even want to see him. I certainly had no intention of going through with the marriage. All I wanted to do was curl up in a ball and die. After the surgery I was flown to the military hospital in Birmingham. I was still a mess—emotionally and physically. I thought of myself as literally only half a person then.

'But the others—the other patients, amputees—wouldn't let me give up. They pushed me and tormented me until I was determined to damn well show them I could—and would—walk again. Months later, Davie came back to visit. I still couldn't bear him to see me but he begged.' Her eyes softened. 'It was Nick who persuaded me in the end.' She glanced over at Nick and Tiggy followed her gaze. He was leaning against the wall, his eyes half-closed so she couldn't read his expression. 'Nick told me that if I didn't say goodbye properly to Davie, if I didn't tell him I couldn't be with him face to face, I would regret it for the rest of my life.'

Still Nick said nothing but a hard lump was forming in Tiggy's throat. Had he ever thought of how they'd never really said goodbye? Had he regretted the way things had ended between them?

'I gave in. And as soon as I saw Davie walking towards me, I knew. If he still wanted me in his life, I would never send him away again. I told him that the years would be hard, that I couldn't promise I wouldn't get depressed or angry, but if he was prepared to put up with all of that, if he could truly accept me, this new, broken me, I would do everything in my power to make him happy.'

Tiggy's chest was so tight she was finding it hard to breathe.

'What did he say?'

A smile lit Hazel's face. 'He said he loved me. Whole or not, he would never stop loving me, that being without me had been hell on earth. Then I guess we cried a lot.' Her smile grew wider. 'We have a daughter now. She's two. And I'm in training for the Paralympics. I dream sometimes that I'm whole again, but to be honest I couldn't be happier.'

Tiggy blinked the tears away. Had she been in Hazel's situation, would she have had a fraction of her courage?

'This is who I am now. I tour the country speaking to amputees, especially young amputees. I train, I have my daughter and I have my husband. I wouldn't trade any of it to get my legs back.'

Tiggy smiled. 'I think you're just the person Jo needs to chat to. Come on, let's find her parents and introduce you.'

Half an hour later Hazel was sitting on the chair next to Jo's bed talking softly. Jo was still staring up at the ceiling but Tiggy knew from the way her head was cocked that she was listening. It wouldn't happen overnight, there were bound to be ups and downs, but she knew that Jo was out of danger. This remarkable, courageous young woman would see to it.

Jo's parents were waiting by the door with Nick. They held out their hands to Tiggy. 'We don't know how to thank you. Where did you find Hazel?'

Tiggy looked directly at Nick, ignoring the warning shake of his head. 'It's not me you have to thank, it's Dr Casey here.'

Tiggy had to leave Hazel with the family to go to A and E to start her shift. She walked Nick to the front entrance and held out her car keys. She couldn't trust herself to speak.

He ignored her proffered hand. His eyes were dark. 'No, thanks. I think I'll walk.'

She didn't say all the things she wanted to, like 'Are you sure you'll be all right?' or 'Thank you' or 'Take care'. Nick was who he was. A grown man with the right to make his own decisions, however much she didn't agree with, or understand, them.

She nodded and before she realised what she was going to do she stood on tiptoe and kissed him full on the mouth.

CHAPTER TEN

LATER THAT NIGHT Tiggy lay in bed, wondering if she was going completely crazy.

Hadn't she spent the last six years trying to forget him? Yet here she was longing for him with every damn cell in her body. How sad, pathetic and weak was that?

The wind whispered in the trees outside and she shivered. She got up to close the window and that's when she heard it. A cry, a shout?

It was coming from Nick's room.

She was in his room, kneeling by his bed, before she had time to think.

His naked limbs were tangled in the sheets and he was thrashing wildly, the sweat running down his forehead. She'd witnessed his nightmares before but never like this. Had she been right to worry all along? Was this a sign of the shrapnel moving in his spine? And, if so, could his uncontrolled movements shift the shrapnel and do more damage?

She placed a hand against his damp forehead and pushed the hair from his eyes. 'Shh, Nick. It's me, Tiggy. Everything's all right.'

She tried to press him gently back down onto the mattress but, still in the throes of his nightmare, he pushed her away. 'No! Go! You have to get away!'

Unable to bear seeing him like this, she lay down next to him and wrapped her arms around his waist. 'Wake up, Nick. You're safe now.'

His eyelids flickered. 'Tiggy?' He buried his face in her neck. 'You're really here?'

'Yes, it's me. You've been having a bad dream. But that's all it is, a bad dream.'

When his eyes opened his pupils were large and unfocussed. Her heart banged against her ribs. Was it just a nightmare or was there something else going on?

'Talk to me, Nick. Are you all right?'

'Tiggy,' he groaned, his voice thick, and as he gazed at her, his eyes regained focus and he whispered again. 'My Tiggy.'

Relieved that whatever was tormenting him was receding, she laid her head on his chest. The heat of his body burned through the thin material of her camisole. Despite her terror for him, she was aware of every hard muscle against her. 'Yes. It's me,' she said again. 'I'm here.'

His hands moved in her hair. 'I was dreaming… You were hurt. I was trying to save you… I couldn't get to you.'

'Shh,' she soothed. 'I'm safe. I'm here and I'm safe. You were having a nightmare. Go back to sleep now.'

His hands dropped to the curve of her waist, resting for a moment before moving on as if he needed to convince himself she was really beside him.

His touch sent shock waves of heat through her and, as she felt the familiar torturous ache of desire, she fought the urge to turn and press her body into his.

Tentatively his hand moved under her camisole and when she made no attempt to stop him he moved upwards to her breasts. Her nipples hardened under his exploring fingers and she moaned softly. His breathing was as ragged as hers as he pulled her against him. 'God, Tiggy, you're so beautiful.'

Her treacherous body melted into his. She knew, of course she knew, that she should unwrap his arms from around her and walk away, but she could no more do that than fly to the moon. Every fibre of her body ached for him. But more than that she wanted to comfort him, ease his mental anguish. He was facing a future where he could be paralysed, if he survived.

Immediately, she pushed the thought away. She mustn't think like that.

But one night. What could one last night hurt?

'Are you sure, Tiggy?' he murmured into her hair. 'Because if you don't stop me now...'

She arched her body into his and lifted her face. 'I'm sure,' she whispered. If he rejected her now she didn't know if she could bear it.

He brought his lips down and kissed her as if he was drowning and she was his salvation. She kissed him back, inhaling the familiar scent of him, soap and spice, revelling in the taste of him, the hardness of his lips.

His hands slipped further down her back until he was cupping her bottom. Apart from her camisole she was only wearing panties, and using his thumbs he quickly divested her of those.

As his weight shifted on the bed and he rose over her, a shaft of moonlight settled on his scars. She put a hand to his chest. 'Wait, Nick.'

With a groan of dismay he jerked away from her and sank back on the bed. But she bent over him removing the arm he'd flung across his eyes. 'Your injury. We need to be careful. Take it gently.'

He looked at her, his expression fathomless. Black diamonds, she thought as she covered his body with her own. 'Stay still. Let me.'

As they moved together in a slow and gentle dance, it was everything she remembered and more. Every time he tried to take control she would stop him with a kiss until he was content to match her careful rhythm. After they climaxed, crying out in unison, she sank into him and he held her, stroking her hair until she fell asleep.

The next morning Tiggy crept out of bed, careful not to wake Nick. She'd be driving him to the hospital later for his pre-op assessment, and after last night she wanted him to get as much rest as possible.

As she made some coffee she hummed. She blushed every time she thought about the passion they'd shared. It was as if they'd never been apart from each other. No, that was wrong, it was just like when they'd first started sleeping together. That same desperate need, the same instinctive understanding of what each other's bodies craved... that same mind-blowing release.

Maybe they could get back together, maybe they could put the past behind them, and once Nick had recovered from his operation...start all over again? This time she would make him talk to her. Perhaps, in a few months, discuss having a baby.

Whoa! She was getting way ahead of herself. Nothing, essentially, had really changed.

She placed two mugs on a tray while she waited for the coffee to percolate.

It wouldn't be easy. Nick might have mellowed but he was still the challenging, complicated man he'd always been. She wouldn't love him the way she did if he wasn't.

She still loved him.

Of course she did.

She'd never, not even for a single second, stopped. She'd been mad at him, almost hated him at times, but she'd never stopped loving him.

And she never would. She was bound to Nick for all her life. No question. Child or no child, life-threatening condition or not, he was the missing part of her soul. Was there some way they could find their way back to each other again?

She picked up the tray and walked to his room. The bed was empty and Nick, dressed once more in his jeans, was looking out of the window. She couldn't help the thrill of desire that ran up her spine when her eyes came to rest at the small dent at the base of his spine. Only hours before she'd been kissing him just there, knowing it always drove him crazy. And she had every intention of doing it again.

'Nick?' she said. 'I thought I'd bring you coffee in bed, but I see—'

Before she could finish, he'd spun around, his expression so remote it stopped the words in her throat.

'What's wrong? Why are you looking at me like that?' she managed at last.

He raked a hand through his hair. 'Last night. It was a mistake. I'm sorry. I took advantage. It won't happen again.'

Her pulse was beating in her temple as she placed the tray on the bedside table. 'You didn't take advantage, Nick. I wanted to just as much as you did.'

He groaned. 'Tiggy, don't say any more. You did what any caring woman would do. You gave comfort when it was needed.'

'That's hogwash, Nick. You can't possibly think I slept with you because I thought you might die. I have no doubt that you're going to be fine—just fine.' That wasn't exactly true, but she wasn't about to admit it.

'Then it was just one night? You don't expect…? You're not thinking that we might get back together again? Because that's not going to happen.'

It was as if the bottom was falling out of her world. Of course, that's exactly what she'd been thinking.

'Why not?' she said. 'When this is all over perhaps we could…'

He laughed, a cold, mirthless sound, his eyes empty, bottomless pools. 'I couldn't do marriage six years ago, Tigs. What makes you think anything's changed?'

Her hands were shaking and she laced her fingers together in case he noticed. 'I see,' she said quietly, unbearably aware of the tremor in her voice.

'I still care about you, Tiggy, you know that. And you're still the sexiest woman I have ever known, but that's it. If I let you believe otherwise I'd be a bigger swine than I already am.'

Red rage swept through her. Of all the patronising things to say! She had been such an idiot to think, even for a second, that they had a chance. 'Of course you haven't changed, Nick. Sex is all that matters to you. That and the admiration of your troops. You're still the selfish, self-centred man I married. You only care about satisfying your own needs. Well, let me tell you, I've changed. Last night was…was just meaningless sex.'

She knew she was lashing out to hide her own pain but she didn't care. She searched around for something else to say, knowing but uncaring that she wanted to hurt him the way he'd hurt her.

'You're not a man who does relationships, you think I don't know that? It's the men out there who use up all your sympathy, all your heart. It's not their fault that there's nothing left for the rest of us.'

Her throat was so tight with the need to cry she could

hardly swallow. 'Here's your coffee. I hope you choke on it.' And with that last, remarkably mature comment she stalked out of the room.

Nick had to stop himself from going after her. He'd hurt her, hurt her badly, and she was the last person in the world who deserved it.

What had he been thinking when he'd made love to her last night? The truth was he hadn't been thinking, not with his head anyway. When he'd woken from whatever nightmare had had him in its grip this time and had found her bending over him, her silky curls a whisper on his chest, the smell of the honey and jasmine of her perfume, his reaction had been immediate. And uncontrollable.

He'd dreamt of holding her so many times it had been impossible to push her away. So selfishly, his mind filled with his need for her, he'd accepted what she'd so innocently offered, without thinking about the consequences.

But when he'd woken up to find her gone, the sheet where her body had lain still warm from her skin, the scent of her still on his fingers, filling his senses, cold rational thought had returned. Too late perhaps, but it had come anyway.

He would give anything to be with Tiggy again. And it would be so different this time—but, hell, he couldn't. He had nothing to offer her. He had even less to offer than when he'd left her six years ago. In a few days' time he could be paralysed—or dead.

He cursed under his breath. She was right. He'd behaved in the worst possible way. He was a selfish bastard. But not selfish enough that he would tie her to a man who might end up having to be cared for. He'd done the wrong thing by agreeing to come home with her, but he could do the right thing now. He had to leave her to get on with her life. Without him.

Even if the thought of that ripped him in two.

Tiggy dried her eyes, resenting the fact they were still red. She had stayed in the shower for almost an hour. Every time she thought she had herself together, she'd start sobbing again. It was almost as if she was finally grieving for Nick.

Now she knew she'd always been waiting for him to see sense and come back to her. Now she knew with absolute certainty that it wasn't going to happen.

She sniffed loudly and pressed a cold cloth to her red-rimmed eyes. She was damned if she was going to let him see how much he'd hurt her. It was some while before she was ready to leave the bathroom. She'd promised to drive Nick to the hospital and that's what she'd do.

It didn't matter what he said, she was still his wife and she would be with him, at least until after the surgery. After that—supposing he came through—he was on his own. And if he didn't? She wouldn't think about that now. She was barely managing to cope with her thoughts as it was. She would face it if and when it had to be faced, and not a moment before.

When she was dressed she went to tell Nick it was time to leave, but he wasn't in his room or the sitting room.

Then she noticed the note on the table.

She picked it up. As she read it, her heart disintegrated.

Dear Tiggy,
I've taken a taxi to hospital.
I think it's best if we don't see each other again.
I'm sorry about last night. Sorry for all the pain I've

caused you. If I could change the past, or who I am,
to make you happy, I would.
But I can't.
Take care.
Nick.

Tiggy stared at the letter before crumpling it into a ball. Where did Nick get off telling her what she could and couldn't do? And in a note!

She deserved more than that.

She was done with him treating her like she didn't have a mind of her own.

Cold fury was rapidly taking over. Who the hell did he think he was? What gave him the right to waltz in and out of her life when it suited him?

If he thought she was going to accept a note as a good-bye, he had another think coming. And she planned to tell him so.

But first there was someone she needed to talk to.

CHAPTER ELEVEN.

'Why didn't you tell me this before?'

Tiggy's mum slid a cup of tea in front of her.

'Because…I thought you'd disapprove,' Tiggy admitted. 'I know you're angry with Nick. I didn't know how to tell you he was back.'

Her mother pushed a lock of hair from Tiggy's face before sitting down opposite her.

As always, when Tiggy was in trouble she found herself turning to her mum. It didn't matter that she was thirty-six and should be able to work out her own problems. Somehow everything felt clearer once she'd talked it over with her mother.

'It doesn't matter what I think. And, for the record, I'm not angry with Nick. It takes two to make, or break, a marriage.'

Her words had Tiggy sitting bolt upright. 'You can't possibly think that the break-up was anything to do with me,' she spluttered. 'No way. He was the one who put an end to it.'

Her mother raised an eyebrow and Tiggy's cheeks reddened. Whose side was her mother on?

'Well, I may have left, but I always meant to go back. I mean I did, the next day. But he'd gone. He didn't even try to get me back. God, Mum, he didn't even wait a day before he was off.'

'But the fact is you did leave first.'

Tiggy jumped to her feet. 'I can't believe you're saying that!'

'For heaven's sake, Tiggy, sit down. I'm not saying that you were to blame for the break-up, but I'm not saying he was either. All I am saying is it takes two. You were always stubborn. And I always thought there was more to Nick than met the eye. That man is hiding something.'

'You never said!'

'It wasn't my place. You were his wife. It was for the two of you to work things out.'

'What do you mean, hiding something?' It was so close to what Tiggy had suspected that her heart sank. 'You mean like an affair?'

Her mother shot her a look of disbelief. 'No, of course not that. You couldn't have known your husband as well as you think you did if you believed that for one moment. Nick may be a complicated man but he's an honest one. It was clear to everyone who saw you two together that the man worshipped the ground you walked on.'

Tiggy sat back down at the table. 'Worshipped the ground I walked on? Really, Mum? Then how do you explain why he shut me out all the time? And...' her voice hitched '...never came back to me? If he really cared for me, why didn't he fight for our marriage? I loved him so much.'

'It seems to me, darling girl, that perhaps Nick isn't the man you wanted him to be. Perhaps he wasn't right for you. Not if you wanted him to be something he couldn't be.'

'You are so wrong. I didn't want Nick to change. I loved him and all that he was.'

But despite her protestations a horrible little thought

was snaking its way inside her head. Could her mother be right? Had she been at least partly at fault? Had she given up too soon?

'Do you still love him?' her mother asked.

He had broken her heart and was still breaking it, so there was only one answer.

'Yes. I'll never stop loving him.'

Her mother sighed. 'What are you going to do now?'

'Nothing. What can I do? He doesn't want me in his life. He told me so this morning.'

Her mother reached out a hand across the table. 'You hear what he's *saying*, but what is he *feeling*? Do you really know for sure?'

'How can I know? He doesn't talk to me!'

'Then the question, surely, is why not? Has he ever said he doesn't love you any more?'

'No...'

'Is it possible you gave up on him too soon and not the other way around?'

Tiggy stood up. 'All I know is that I won't let him treat me as if I don't matter.'

Her mother arched an eyebrow. 'Well, then, isn't it time you told him so?'

CHAPTER TWELVE

NICK GLANCED UP to find Tiggy bearing down on him like some sort of avenging angel. He could tell from the set of her mouth that she was seriously hacked off. He groaned. He should have known she would do what she wanted to do regardless of how much he tried to prevent her.

He looked around for an escape route but Tiggy was between him and the only way out of the ward. Besides, he was confined to bed. He'd been given his pre-med a few minutes earlier and was already feeling groggy.

'So,' she said, her eyes glinting dangerously, 'at least you turned up for your op.'

'Of course I did,' he said. 'Once I make a decision I stick to it.'

'Why didn't you let me know where you were last night?'

'I was in a hotel. I thought it best.' He'd walked away from her because he'd believed it was the right thing to do. Even if it had taken every ounce of his willpower. The thought that he'd never see her again had torn him apart, and only the knowledge that he'd been doing the right thing had stopped him from turning up on her doorstep and taking her back into his arms.

'Well, I'm here to tell you something.' She wagged a

finger at him. 'Don't you ever decide what's best for me. *I* make that decision.'

Her words made him smile. All he'd ever wanted to do was protect Tiggy. But she was right. She had coped, more than coped, in the years they'd been apart. He'd clearly underestimated her. Then—and now.

'I'm not finished yet, so you can lose the smile. When you're discharged from the hospital, you're coming home with me.' She held up a hand as if to ward off his protests. 'No arguing. As you pointed out, the house still half belongs to you.' She dropped her voice. 'We meant something to each other once, Nick. As you say, that's in the past, but I'm still your wife. For better or worse. You can go as soon as you're on your feet. I won't…' He was getting increasingly woozy but were those tears in her eyes? 'I won't hold you back from leaving, I promise, but until then you're my responsibility. Get it?' She leaned over the bed and kissed him on the lips. 'Get through this, Nick. Do whatever you have to, but get through this.'

A short while later Nick was wheeled down to theatre. The operation, as the surgeon, Dr Wiseman, had explained, would take a few hours. He couldn't say exactly how long as that would depend on what he discovered when he opened up Nick's back. In the meantime, Tiggy was welcome to wait in the relatives' room.

The waiting was the worst part. What if something went wrong? If Nick died on the table, how would she bear it?

But that wasn't going to happen. She had to believe that the operation would be a success.

She would wait, make sure he was all right. And then? As she'd promised, as soon as the hospital was happy, she'd take him home until he was back on his feet. After that? She didn't know.

She heard a soft footstep and looked up to find her mother, father and two brothers standing in the doorway.

'Mum, Dad? Charlie, Alan? What are you doing here?'

They smiled down at her. 'Did you think for one moment we were going to let you do this on your own?' her mother asked. And then before she knew it she was in the safe cocoon of her family's arms.

It was several hours later before Luke came to tell her that the operation was over. Her family made a small half-circle around her as they waited for Luke to speak.

'It went better than we hoped,' he said. 'We managed to remove the shrapnel without too much difficulty. We won't know if there's residual nerve damage for a while, and your husband will be in ITU for a few hours before we transfer him to the ward, but…' he smiled at Tiggy '…I think it's safe to say that he's going to be fine.'

Relief made her feel dizzy. Nick was okay. That was all that really mattered.

'Can I see him?' Tiggy asked.

'Yes of course, although I'm afraid you're the only one allowed in at this stage.'

Tiggy said goodbye to her family, promising to phone them later, and hurried along to ITU. Steeling herself for what she'd find, she walked briskly towards him.

As she'd expected, there were lines everywhere and Nick looked pale. To her relief, he wasn't on a ventilator.

She sat down next to the bed and studied him, noticing how the lines had deepened on his forehead and around his eyes.

Her heart tightened. He'd hate her to see him like this. That was part of the problem in their marriage. He'd never needed her—not in the way she'd needed him. And whatever had happened out there in Afghanistan, whatever had been eating at his soul, he hadn't been able to share that either. For the first time she realised that what her mother had said was true—she'd failed Nick as much as he'd failed her.

Could this be their second chance? She didn't know if the wounds they'd inflicted on each other were too deep to ever heal and she didn't even know if Nick could ever love her again, but what she did know was that she wasn't going to give up on him this time without a fight.

CHAPTER THIRTEEN

WHEN TIGGY RETURNED that evening, she was delighted to find that Nick had been taken out of ITU and put in High Dependency instead. Luke was standing at the end of his bed, studying his chart.

'How is he?' Tiggy whispered.

'He's doing great. He's so fit I suspect he'll be back on his feet much sooner than we imagined.'

Tiggy smiled. 'I have no doubt of it.

Nick's eyes flickered open. 'Hi, Tigs,' he said drowsily. 'You look cute.' Then he fell asleep again.

'I'll leave you two alone,' Luke said. 'You know how to call for help if you need it.'

Tiggy remained by Nick's bed, unable to bring herself to leave him even to go for a coffee, until the nurses insisted that visiting was over.

The next morning she was told he'd continued to make such good progress that he'd been transferred onto the surgical ward. He was still on a saline drip but was conscious.

As she approached, he threw back the covers.

'Just what do you think you're doing?' Tiggy asked, pressing him back against the pillows.

'I need to pee.'

'Then you'll have to use a bottle. You're not allowed out of bed until tomorrow.'

'You expect me to pee in a bottle?' He couldn't have sounded more outraged had she suggested he rob a bank.

'I'll fetch one for you, shall I?' Now she knew he was going to be okay, Tiggy was beginning to enjoy herself.

He glared at her. 'If you think for one minute I'm about to lie here while you help me use a bottle, think again.'

'I'll get one of the nurses, then.'

Nick looked as if he was about to argue, but then sank back on the pillows. 'I suppose if I have to.'

'But the nurses are busy...' she smiled down at him '... so after you've finished with the bottle, I'll be giving you your bed bath.'

'You have got to be kidding!'

'Nope. 'Fraid not.'

Nick was prevented from saying anything in reply by the arrival of the nurse.

Tiggy fetched a basin of warm water and waited until the nurse had taken away the bottle before she popped behind the screens.

Nick studied her warily. 'You're not serious about this bed-bath stuff.'

'Perfectly serious.'

She plonked the basin on the locker. 'Now, we can do this the easy way or the hard way, as they say in the movies.' She was definitely beginning to enjoy herself.

'What's the easy way?'

'That's where you lie still and let me do what I need to.'

A slow smile crossed his face. 'I think I've heard you say that before.'

She bit back a smile. She wasn't about to admit that the night he was talking about was imprinted in her memory.

'And what's the hard way?'

'The hard way is when you resist—or try to help me.'

'Let's go for the easy way, then.'

She was beginning to have her doubts. It had seemed a good way of getting back at Nick, but she hadn't expected him to capitulate so quickly.

She unbuttoned his pyjama top. He'd never worn them, preferring to sleep naked.

Mustn't think of him naked.

The lower part of his torso was heavily bandaged. Tiggy's mouth dried. She dipped the facecloth in the water and wrung it out. She washed his face, feeling the rasp of his beard through the cloth.

'You could do with a shave,' she said mildly.

'Not sure I could trust you that far.' He grinned. He'd always used an open razor to shave.

'You'll do until tomorrow.'

She raised each arm in turn and soaped and rinsed. All the while he lay there, watching her with sleepy, amused brown eyes.

It turned into a game, both waiting to see just how far she'd go. She soaped his calves in turn, lifting them gently so as not to cause him any pain, but when it came to washing his upper thighs she couldn't resist glancing at him. His eyes were glinting and he had a half-smile on his lips. She rinsed the cloth and made to pull his pyjama trousers down. Suddenly his hand snaked out and grabbed hers. 'That's as far as you go, sweetheart,' he groaned.

She smiled down at him. 'Lost your nerve?' She covered him with the sheet again and tucked him in. 'At last, payback for the time you humiliated me at Camp Bastion. Remember? The press-ups?'

He looked at her through slitted eyes. 'I think we're quits, don't you?'

Grinning, Nick watched Tiggy stomp out of the room. God, he'd missed her. Missed her spark, missed the way she lifted her chin whenever she was mad, missed the feel of her hands on his body.

He'd missed everything about her.

And now?

He'd let her go in the first place because he'd wanted her to have the life she deserved. But she hadn't found someone else; hadn't had the children she desired. And why not? Had he hurt her so badly she had never let herself trust again? And he'd hurt her all over again by making love to her and walking away. So why the hell was she giving him the time of day? Pity? A sense of guilt for a failed marriage? Ridiculous—and yet what other explanation was there? That she still loved him?

Was it possible? A unfamiliar feeling spread through his chest, which he vaguely remembered as unadulterated happiness.

Was there a chance of a future for them?

Because, God help them both, he still loved her. He'd never stopped loving her. No one had ever come close to making him feel the way she had.

And the operation seemed to have been a success. He had his life back. But he didn't want his old life back. Not if it didn't include Tiggy.

CHAPTER FOURTEEN

NICK STOPPED HIS wheelchair outside the front door and frowned.

He had insisted on wheeling himself. Tiggy wasn't even allowed to touch the wheelchair, never mind push him, but the doorway to the house had a small lip.

Nick gritted his teeth, reversed a metre or so down the path and, using his powerful arms, rushed the wheelchair at the door.

To no avail. As before, the wheelchair jammed against the doorway.

'For heaven's sake, Nick,' Tiggy said, exasperated. 'Let me at least get you inside.'

He turned and glared at her. As if it was her fault.

'I can manage,' he insisted.

'Suit yourself,' Tiggy responded mildly, squeezing herself past him and into the house. 'I'm going to make tea. When you get tired of flinging yourself at the immovable object that is the door, let me know.'

Receiving no response, apart from a not-too-well-hidden snarl, she set about doing as she'd said. She filled the kettle and lifted a couple of mugs from the kitchen cupboard.

The tea was made when a satisfied laugh came from

behind her. Nick was in the kitchen, grinning widely. 'Told you I could manage,' he said.

'Would have been easier if you'd allowed me to help.' She nodded at the table. 'Tea's there.'

'We've been through this, Tiggy. I'll have to be in this damn chair for a few days longer but, in the meantime, I will not be treated like—'

'A child?' Tiggy raised one eyebrow at him. 'Because you've been doing a good imitation of one since we left the hospital.'

Nick glared at her again and she glared back. 'Really, Nick, you might be wheelchair-bound but your behaviour over the last couple of hours has been inexcusable.'

To her surprise, the darkness left his eyes and he grinned.

'Trust you to say what you think, Tiggy. You're right. I have been behaving badly.'

No worse than you've behaved in the past, she added silently. Damn stubborn man.

'But don't you see? If I were one of my men, I would give no quarter and neither would they expect any. If they can come to terms with having to learn to walk all over again, so can I.'

'I'm quite sure they accept help when it's offered.'

'They accept help when they can't manage for themselves. I'll do no less.'

Tiggy shrugged, pretending a nonchalance she was far from feeling. 'Suit yourself.'

Nick's expression darkened. 'At least there's a good chance *I'll* get back on my feet,' he muttered.

'For God's sake, Nick, do you have to flay yourself alive every time you think of one of those poor men? The war isn't your fault. What happened to them isn't your fault. You've spent the best part of your career doing your damnedest to keep them alive, to keep them from losing their limbs, to keep them whole.'

'I did have help, Tiggy,' he responded dryly.

'Then what about Luke? You saved his life. You saved his leg. If it hadn't been for you, God knows what would have happened to him.' She softened her voice. 'He told me you're the reason he became a doctor. Did you know that?'

'It seems to me that Luke tells you way too much.'

When they had finished their drinks Tiggy picked up the mugs and placed them in the sink.

'Do you want to lie down for a bit? You could use the sofa in the sitting room.'

'I thought we agreed you weren't going to treat me as a patient. If I want to lie down, I'll lie down.'

Tiggy whirled round. 'Okay. Suit yourself. You can rot in that chair for all I care. I'm going for a run.'

By the time she returned, she'd exercised away her irritation with Nick. The truth was she wasn't so much angry with him as unsure of how to be around him.

Nick was sitting in the armchair with his feet up on a stool, watching football.

'How was your run?' he asked with a smile.

Anyone would think she'd imagined the grumpy individual of earlier.

'It was good. Perhaps when you're up to it we can go together?'

Nick narrowed his eyes. 'Give me three weeks.'

'Three weeks! You're crazy to think you'll be running in three weeks.'

'Just watch me,' he said.

Over the next few days they settled into a routine. Tiggy prepared breakfast before she left for work and Nick always made it to the kitchen before it was on the table.

She suspected he set his alarm for six to give himself time to get dressed.

They would eat together then he would shoo her off to work, insisting she leave the breakfast dishes for him.

By the time she returned from the hospital he'd have a simple dinner ready or, more often, a take-away ordered, and they'd sit at the kitchen table and he would ask her about work. When she suggested she take him out in his wheelchair, he was aghast.

'No way is anyone going to see me in this contraption,' he protested. 'I'm not leaving this house until I can walk.'

'Then you'd better keep practising,' she said.

The first weekend she slept late and woke up to the smell of coffee. Nick was at the kitchen table, looking pleased with himself.

'Notice anything?' he asked.

'Yep. Seems you can finally make coffee.'

'You haven't tasted it yet.'

And, right enough, as soon as she took a sip she was transported back to the camp and the horrible coffee from the mess tent. She tipped hers down the sink and set about making another, decent pot.

Nick pretended to be offended. 'Hey, do you have any idea how long that took me to make?'

For the first time she noticed he wasn't in his wheel-chair.

'You walked in here?' she asked incredulously.

'I wouldn't say walked exactly. More like stumbled. But, yes, it won't be long before we can go running together.'

'Don't overdo it, Nick.'

He frowned at her. 'In my book, there's no such thing as overdoing it.'

She ignored him and went to sit at the table. 'In that

case, have you made plans about what you're going to do when you're completely fit?'

'I have to appear before the medical board in a few weeks. They'll make a decision about my fitness to continue with the army then.'

Although his tone was nonchalant, a muscle twitched in his jaw, the way it always did when he was annoyed about something.

'What if they say no? What will you do then?'

He raised his eyes. 'They won't say no. I'll make sure of it.'

'You don't have to stay in the army. As I said before, someone of your experience could walk into a consultant post in any hospital in the UK.' She paused. 'Would it still be so terrible to be a civilian doctor?'

He shook his head. 'It's still tough out there. The men need me.'

'Don't you think you've done enough?'

He stared into the distance. 'Who can say what is enough? It never seems to be enough.' He leaned forward. 'Almost every week we're coming up with innovations that save more lives. You know they used to talk about the golden hour? Now they talk about the platinum ten minutes. If we can get the best medical care to the men within that time—assuming they're still alive—we can usually save them.'

'And it's people like you who have made it possible.'

He didn't seem to be listening to her. He seemed to have gone somewhere inside his head.

'When they stopped me going out on patrol with the men, I was furious. I knew that they needed the most experienced surgeon possible to be right there, alongside them. But once I got to consultant level the bloody command said I was too valuable to risk. Going out with the rapid response team was the next best thing.' He was speaking so softly she had to strain to hear him. 'It was bad enough when the injuries were shrapnel or bullet wounds but when they started using IEDs…' He shook his head. 'The injuries were more severe than anything we'd ever seen before.'

He was telling her more than he had in all the years they'd been married.

'But you saved them. Most of them.'

'Not all of them. Remember the soldier we lost when you were there?' When Tiggy nodded he continued. 'There was a young female army medic. She was one of the first women to go out on patrol with the men. She was only nineteen. I went out with the RRT when we got the call. We didn't know what to expect. You know how difficult it is to get the right information back at base. Anyway, by the time we got to her, it was too late. All I could do was hold her. She died in my arms. All the time she was dying I was thinking of you. Thinking of our lives back here. Knowing that you wanted me to give it up so we could have a normal life. I also knew I couldn't. As long as these men and women were out there, I had to be there too.'

'Why didn't you talk to me about it?'

'I didn't want to bring all that home. When I was with you I wanted to think of nothing but you. But I couldn't get the images out of my head. I couldn't rest at home, not when I knew I should be with them.'

'I thought you regretted marrying me,' she said sadly.

He raised his eyes again and she reeled back from the anguish she saw there.

'I did regret marrying you,' he said. 'I loved you, but I couldn't be with you. Why didn't you divorce me? My solicitor sent the papers.'

'Perhaps because for me marriage is forever,' she whispered. Although that wasn't the true reason. At least, not all of it. She knew now she'd never given up hope that one day he'd come back to her. That weekend, when she'd run away to her mother's, she'd been so sure he would come after her, tell her that he needed her more than the army, but he hadn't. When she'd returned home, determined to talk to him, to find a way to be together, he'd gone and had taken most of his belongings with him.

It had been then that she'd broken down. But she'd refused to call him or write. She wouldn't beg. If Nick no longer loved her, it was better that he'd left.

But it had taken years before she'd given up hope that he'd come back. All these years just one little sign from him would have been enough. But that sign had never come.

She turned away from him. 'You were the one who really left in the end, remember?'

'I thought it was best.'

'Best for whom?'

'You wanted a baby, Tiggy. I couldn't. Not then, perhaps not ever.'

'It wasn't a baby I wanted, Nick. I mean, of course I wanted our child, but only because I wanted something that was part of both of us. Most of all I wanted us to be a normal family. You, me, our child. Our children. What was so wrong with that?'

He shook his head. 'It wasn't that I didn't want them too. I did, but not when... It was crazy in Afghanistan back then, Tiggy. I saw too many young men die, men with young babies. Men leaving women to cope alone. Just like my mother had to cope with me. I couldn't do that to you.'

She pushed herself away from the table. 'As I said before, it wasn't something for you to decide on your own. You didn't have faith in us. You didn't have faith in me. I was stronger than you gave me credit for. If anything had happened to you it would have broken me, of course it would, but I would have found a way to go on. And if we'd had a child, at least I would have had a part of you.'

He looked up at her. 'I know that now, Tigs. But I thought I was doing the best thing for you.'

She shook her head. 'That's not good enough. If you really loved me, Nick, nothing would have kept you away.' She turned away. 'If you'll excuse me, I have stuff I need to do.'

CHAPTER FIFTEEN

TIGGY CAME BACK from work on Monday to the astonishing sight of Nick doing pirouettes in his wheelchair with both twins on his lap.

'Faster!' Chrissie squealed.

'Go round again,' Melody, the quieter twin, insisted.

'What on earth is going on? Where did you two come from?'

The twins, instead of leaping into her arms the way they usually did, stayed where they were, as if glued to Nick.

'Hi, sis.' Her brother Charlie appeared in the door of the sitting room. 'We were on our way back from doing some shopping in the city and thought we'd pop in. Mum said Nick was staying with you.'

He scooped up a twin in each arm and plonked them on the floor. 'That's enough, you two. Give Uncle Nick a break.'

'Uncle Nick?' Tiggy mouthed at her brother out of sight of Nick and the twins.

'I thought I would take Nick down to the pub for a pint if you don't mind keeping an eye on these two rascals. It's been a while.'

'I don't imagine Nick wants to go to the pub.' Behind Nick she shook her head.

'What you doing, Aunty Tiggy?' Chrissie asked. 'Why are you shaking your head at Daddy?'

'You never told us we had an Uncle Nick,' Melody complained. 'And he's got a wheelchair.'

'Tiggy thinks I can't be trusted in a pub, Charlie,' Nick said. He smiled ruefully. 'Had one too many a few nights ago.'

Charlie and Nick had always got along. They had rarely been on leave at the same time, but on the rare occasions they had met, they had always been relaxed in each other's company. Once they had even gone on a climbing trip together. Charlie had been shocked and annoyed with Tiggy when he'd heard that they'd separated, and had said so. After that, she'd refused to discuss the subject with him.

Nick was getting to his feet, having pulled his crutches towards him.

'A pint sounds great,' he said. 'It may take us a while to get there, though.'

'I'll give you a lift,' Tiggy offered.

Nick frowned at her. 'No,' he said. 'A walk sounds good to me.'

'If you're not back in an hour or two,' Tiggy warned, 'I'll be down to drag you both out of there.'

As soon as they'd left, Tiggy organised the children with some colouring pens and paper and set about making dinner.

When the men still hadn't returned an hour later she fed the twins. Then she telephoned her sister-in-law to let her know what was happening.

'Nick is back living with you?' Alice couldn't have sounded more aghast if Tiggy had said she was shacking up with Genghis Khan.

'It's a long story,' Tiggy said. 'I'll tell you all about it when I see you next.'

'But—'

'Sorry, I have to go.' Tiggy knew if she didn't get off the phone Alice would insist on a blow-by-blow account. On the other hand, the family had probably discussed it around the kitchen table ad nauseam.

'Can we play dressing-up?' Melody asked, interrupting her musings.

Tiggy smiled. 'Of course you can.'

When the girls had scuttled off to find the box of old clothes she kept for them to dress up in, she poured herself a glass of wine and wandered into the sitting room. Charlie was a traitor. But, then, she'd never talked about the break-up with her family.

When it had all started to go wrong she had been too embarrassed, too frightened to tell them she was losing Nick. There had also been her deep-rooted sense of loyalty to him and the conviction that whatever was wrong in their marriage had been between them and no one else. When Nick had moved out she'd avoided her family for weeks and had then simply told them that things hadn't worked out.

The door banged and the sounds of laughter drifted in on the night air.

'Where are you, sis?' Charlie called out.

She got to her feet. The two of them looked like naughty schoolboys.

'I presume you're ready for supper?' she said.

'How do I look?' a little voice piped up from the doorway. Tiggy spun around and for a moment she couldn't breathe. Melody was wearing her wedding dress. She had totally forgotten she had flung it in the box of dressing-up clothes. Chrissie was holding up the back like a bridesmaid and both girls were beaming from ear to ear.

She turned her head to find Nick's eyes on her.

* * *

Their wedding had been a small affair. They had decided to marry during Nick's leave. When he'd proposed, Tiggy hadn't been able to think of a single reason to delay. Her mother, on the other hand, had been doubtful.

'Isn't it a little soon, darling? You hardly know each other.'

'I know everything I need to, Mum,' Tiggy had replied. 'I love him, he loves me, we want to spend the rest of our lives together. What could be more simple?'

They had been in the kitchen of Tiggy's mother's house, finalizing the details of the wedding.

The crease between her mother's brows had deepened. 'Meeting someone under, let's just say, intense circumstances, can heighten feelings. Marriage can be hard work, darling. Not all men, particularly men like Nick, settle to it easily. Trust me, I know. Your dad was in the army when we met and he hadn't even been in a combat zone.'

'Come on, Mum. Charlie's marriage is fine. And he works in a combat zone!'

'But he knew Alice for several years before they married.'

Tiggy frowned. 'What are you saying, Mum? Don't you believe Nick loves me?'

To be honest, sometimes in the night when Nick hadn't been with her she'd wondered the same thing. Why had Nick fallen in love with her? She was ordinary, nothing special, not even particularly pretty—although Nick had told her repeatedly that he loved the way she looked. And as soon as she'd seen him again the demons of the night had subsided and all her doubts had vanished.

Her mother had sighed. 'I have no doubt he loves you. I just have to see the way he looks at you.'

'Right, then. That's all that matters.'

And their wedding day had been perfect. They'd chosen a country house hotel for the venue—actually, Tiggy had chosen it, as Nick had been back in Afghanistan at the time—and had had a simple ceremony followed by a dinner. Afterwards they had left for a cottage in Yorkshire where they had holed up for the rest of the week, staying in bed all day, only rising to go for walks or get something to eat. It had been the happiest week of Tiggy's life.

Nick was still looking at Melody with a strange look on his face.

'Will you marry me, Uncle Nick?' Melody asked. 'Daddy can be the best man.'

Nick turned his gaze on Tiggy and smiled. 'Sorry, honey. I'm afraid I'm already married.'

After they had eaten and everyone had gone, Tiggy took her wine into the sitting room. Nick was staring into the fire.

'How are you feeling?' Tiggy asked.

'I was thinking about our wedding. I thought I had never seen anyone more beautiful than you that day.'

'You didn't look too shabby yourself.' He'd been in full dress uniform and had looked as sexy as hell.

'What happened to us, Tiggy?'

She set her glass on the table and sat down next to him. 'I don't know, Nick. One minute we were so happy, as if nothing could ever touch us, and the next... I don't know... we were no longer living together.' She laced her hands together to stop them shaking. 'You were so distant that last year. I knew something was wrong, but I didn't know what. I knew even less how to fix it.'

'I don't think you could have.' He turned his dark brown eyes on her. 'It wasn't your fault, Tigs. You did nothing wrong. It was me.'

'Then tell me, Nick. Help me to understand. I always believed a man and wife who loved and trusted each other could share anything and everything—support one another through the bad times as well as the good. Yet you shut me out, Nick, and I couldn't understand it. I began to doubt your love for me and then I began to doubt myself and that the old adage was proving true: marry in haste, repent at leisure. And I felt you regretted our marriage.'

He leaned back on the sofa and studied the ceiling. 'I guess I thought by marrying you I could save myself,' he said after a moment. 'I thought that you would bring me peace, and for a while you did.'

'For a while?'

'The only time I felt truly alive was when I was in Afghanistan. Here with you, it didn't seem real. Nothing seemed real.'

'Oh!' She sucked in a breath as a sharp pain tore through her.

'I never meant to hurt you. It was the last thing I wanted.'

'But you did hurt me.'

'I know.'

'In that case I think you owe it to me to explain what you mean.' However much he didn't want to talk to her, she wasn't going to let him away with that. 'You could have tried talking to me, Nick. You never gave me a chance to try and understand.'

He pushed himself out of the sofa and onto his feet. 'I'm not sure I understood myself. Over the years we were married, things in Afghanistan got worse. It was like living in a capsule. The men, the staff, we were a unit, each relying completely on one another.'

'I know. Remember, I was out there. Did you fall in love with someone else, Nick? Is that what happened? The way you fell in love with me?'

He shook his head. 'No! Of course not. There's never been anyone else but you.'

'Then what?'

'When I was back here with you it was great for the first few days. But being around your family never seemed as real to me as being with the guys. And then after a few days I would get restless. I would wonder what was happening back at camp. Hell, Tiggy I felt guilty. I was with you, safe, and there were men and women out there who needed me.'

'*I* needed you.'

'Not in the way they did.'

She decided to let that pass.

'It hurt me to even think of you, Tiggy. When I was at the camp all I thought about was you—here, in this armchair with a book in your hand, in our bed, going about your day, your normal, peaceful day. And when I was back, it was as if I was infecting our home with the horror of Afghanistan. I wanted to keep it separate. That's why I stopped telling you what was happening out there. It was to protect you.'

'Nick, I didn't need protecting—I was your wife. You shut me out. Don't you see, it was the worst thing you could have done to me? Couldn't you see that when you weren't telling me what was going on, what was happening inside my head was so much worse?'

Her breathing was ragged from the effort of saying the words that had been rattling around in her head for so long.

'You were different. You were happy with our life. I couldn't be. Trust me, Tigs, I tried. And you wanted children. I couldn't see how I could be a father, not while there was a chance I wouldn't be around to see him or her grow up.'

'So you signed up without telling me. Worse, you signed

up for another tour after we'd agreed that you wouldn't. How did you think that made me feel?'

'I never expected the war to last for so long. I thought if I did one final tour, I could settle down. That it would be out of my system. That perhaps then we could have a family. That I could live like a normal person. I was wrong.'

Tiggy got to her feet. 'I suppose I should thank you for being so honest. But it's not the whole truth, is it, Nick? It wasn't just that you wanted to protect me—I could see you were desperate to get back.' She blinked. She wouldn't let him see her cry. 'I'm going to bed.'

He reached out a hand and touched her on the shoulder. 'I would give everything to change the past.' He smiled ruefully. 'But this is who I am, Tiggy. God help me, this is who I am.'

Her heart was a lump of ice. 'I suppose I should thank you for being so honest. But I have to tell you, Nick, none of what you've told me makes me feel any better. You couldn't have loved me. Not really. In the end, I wasn't enough for you, was I?'

The next morning Tiggy stopped by Charlie's house on her way to work. One of the girls had left their favourite doll, and Tiggy knew that as soon as she discovered it was missing there would be tears.

Charlie was in the kitchen, wearing his commercial pilot's uniform. He'd left the army when the twins had been on the way and had joined one of the major airlines. Alice, he explained, had just left to fetch the girls from nursery school. Alan too had been decommissioned and was working with a large engineering firm in Sussex. After years of chasing anything in a skirt, he was engaged to a woman he adored.

Ironically, Tiggy was the only one who hadn't managed to find enduring love.

'Hey, Tiggy,' Charlie said as he straightened his tie. 'Mum's been on the phone, asking me about Nick, and Alice is determined to come and see you. The whole family is buzzing with the news of you and Nick getting back together. Why didn't you tell us?'

'Because we're not back together,' Tiggy said. 'And that's the reason I didn't tell you. I knew you'd all be discussing me.'

Charlie grinned. 'You know what this family's like, sis. One for all, all for one.'

He ruffled her hair. 'For what it's worth, I think it's great news. I always liked Nick.'

'Of course you did. You're both men's men and Nick was someone to go down the pub with, someone to climb bloody mountains with, or whatever else you two got up to.'

Charlie paused. 'I liked him because he was someone who understood what it was really like out there. I liked him because he loved you. But I admit, if he hadn't been on crutches last night I would have punched him for hurting you.'

'Would you?' She stood on tiptoe and kissed her brother on the cheek. 'I have to say he didn't look particularly chastened when you returned him last night.'

'I was going to give him a good ticking-off when I had him on his own, but somehow...' Charlie grinned sheepishly '...we got talking about Afghanistan and then before I knew it, it was time to get back.' He frowned. 'But if you like, when I get back from this trip, I can give him a good talking to.'

Tiggy had to laugh. 'And what are you going to say?

Are you going to tell him that he should go down on his knees and apologise? A bit late for that.'

'What the hell went wrong between you two anyway? You never said.'

'I guess I didn't really know myself. Still don't. But tell me, what did you talk about?'

Charlie poured coffee into two mugs and handed one to Tiggy. 'What do you think we talked about? What we always talk about. I know you women talk about stuff like your innermost feelings and whatever, but men just aren't like that. Most of us prefer to talk about footie. That sort of thing. Or in Nick's and my case, what it was like being on active service. No one who hasn't been there can really understand.'

'I was there,' she reminded him quietly.

'I know. But it's not the same. It's not the same as being there month after month. It's not the same as being fired at and wondering whether you'll be able to hold your nerve or whether you'll turn tail and run. It's not the same as knowing that men and women depend on you to protect them, or rescue them; that if you don't do your job, someone— someone's husband, father, brother sister, even mother— could die.'

'You never talked about it either!'

'No, I didn't, and Alice understood that. I told her some of it, but mostly I kept it to myself. It isn't something you want the people who love you to know. You want to protect them. It's natural.'

'I disagree. Charlie, we're not Victorian women and you're not Victorian men. Don't you see you do us a disservice by thinking like that?'

'I'm afraid you've yet to convince me, sis.' He folded his arms. 'Do you know Nick went to see the families of every man who died under his care? Do you know he visited each man he had operated on to see how they were coping?'

Tiggy sank into a chair. 'No, I didn't. Why didn't he tell me?'

Charlie raised an eyebrow. 'For all the reasons I have just told you. It was horrific out there. When we came back home it was to forget for a while.' He finished his coffee and glanced at his watch. 'Where's Mum? She's looking after the girls for Alice while she goes to the hairdresser. They'll be back any minute and I have to go. But you have to realise, Tiggy, it wasn't all bad out there. I know it's difficult for you to understand but in many ways it was the best time of my life. I have never felt so close to a group of men as I did to my fellow officers. In many ways, I miss it.'

'Sorry, sorry.' Their mother came in and plonked her bag on the table. 'The traffic was horrendous. Some accident, I suspect. Girls and Alice not back yet? Anyway, I'm here now, love, so you can get off. Oh, hello, Tiggy. What are you doing here? I've been wondering why you haven't been round to visit lately.' She peered behind Tiggy. 'And where is Nick?'

Charlie laughed, ruffled Tiggy's hair again and kissed their mother on the cheek. 'I'll leave you to answer the hundred and one questions, Tiggy, but I have to shoot.'

He picked up his captain's cap. His face grew serious. 'Don't give up on him, Tiggy. He's a good man and there aren't many of his sort about.'

CHAPTER SIXTEEN

ALL THAT DAY and in the ones that followed, Tiggy could think of nothing but Nick and whether she should fight for him. Or at least tell him she still loved him. In the end she decided she just couldn't risk it. Not yet. At least, not until Nick gave her some indication that he still cared. She would rather let Nick walk out the door than face being rejected again.

They settled into a routine. She would go to work. While she was at work Nick, determined not to fail his medical, would do his exercises, probably three times as often as he needed to. Before supper they would go for a walk around the neighbourhood. Nick had discarded his crutches for a walking stick and hardly needed to use that any more.

Sometimes they would watch television, more often they would play Scrabble or do the crossword together. In many ways it was as if they were still married—except they weren't sleeping together.

One evening Nick suggested they play poker.

'Are you sure?' she teased. 'Remember, I always beat you.'

He smiled. 'I remember everything. You were so...so different from anyone I'd ever met.'

Instead of fetching the cards, Tiggy curled up in the armchair. She took a deep breath. 'And you were so different from anyone I'd ever met before. I couldn't quite believe at first that you were in love with me, that you wanted to marry me.'

He came across to where she was sitting and took her hands in his. 'I can't believe you didn't know how amazing you are. It was impossible for me *not* to love you. I should have tried harder to keep away from you, but I couldn't.'

'But I wasn't enough for you in the end.'

A shadow crossed his face. 'It wasn't you. Tiggy, you were everything in my life that was good and pure and calm.'

The firelight flickered across his face. In his eyes she saw such terrible pain it almost took her breath away.

'Talk to me, Nick. Please. Charlie told me how you visited the dead men's families, and those you had treated too. Why didn't you tell me that's where you were going? I would have come with you.'

He shook his head.

'I'm not sure I have the answer to that. The last year of our marriage I don't know where my head was. All I knew was that I couldn't bear to be with you.'

It was as if he'd stuck a scalpel into her heart.

'I was aware of that,' she admitted. 'It really hurt.'

'I know,' he said softly. 'I regret that more than I can say. And you're right. I owe you more of an explanation. At first, I couldn't wait to come back to you. I dreamt of you most nights when I was away.' He smiled softly. 'Waking from those dreams and knowing you were hundreds of miles away was hell. But at least you were safe.' He was looking into the distance and not at her. 'Does any of this make sense?'

'I'm not sure. But go on.' Charlie had said much the same thing. Perhaps he was right and whatever the men and women experienced in Afghanistan couldn't be understood except by those who had shared it with them. She'd been there for such a short while and it had become so much worse over the years. She had to try and understand what had driven Nick away from her, even if it broke her heart.

'It was easier to work than think of you. When I was working I could forget everything. I couldn't let myself think of you. If I did I would have allowed your fear to infect me. I had to stay focused. I never knew when the firing would start and I would be needed. I never knew when I might have to go out to the men. I worried constantly about what would happen to you if I died. I was distracted just when I needed to be at my most focused. The men depended on me. It was my job to help bring as many men home as we could.'

A burning cinder from the logs fell on the floor and Nick paused to pick it up and throw it back on the fire. Outside the rain was beating against the windows.

'When they stopped sending me out with the men on patrol, I resented it, although I knew they were right to keep the most senior doctors based at camp.'

He shook his head again. It was almost as if he was talking to himself and had forgotten she was even there. She wanted to reach out to him, to run her hands across his face, to pull him towards her to take his pain into her, but she stayed still, almost scared to breathe lest she stop him talking.

'Then the Taliban started using IEDs. The injuries were horrific. Worse, far worse than anything we'd seen before. Sometimes there was nothing left to save.'

He glanced up at her. 'Are you sure you want to hear this?' he repeated.

Tiggy nodded.

'I had to shut down my mind to do what I needed to do. I stopped thinking that the war was just. I simply wanted us all to get the hell out of there and for the carnage to stop. But in the meantime I had to stay. I saw them, you know—the new recruits as they arrived. Some of them boys still.

'When I came home on leave I couldn't relax. I felt guilty every moment I was away from there. Every time I closed my eyes I would imagine a soldier being brought in, needing my help. And I wasn't there.'

'What about the other doctors and nurses—just as experienced and dedicated as you? It wasn't as if you were abandoning the men. And you needed time off.'

He smiled ruefully. 'I know, at least in my head I knew, but I didn't really believe it. I guess I had started to believe in my own myth. That if I was there, I could save more men.'

'They always did believe you were some kind of lucky talisman.'

'Rightly or wrongly, I began to resent every minute I wasn't at the camp. Being home, being with you, no longer felt real. It was as if I was playing a part in a kind of charade.'

'That's what our marriage was to you?'

'It wasn't you. It was never you. I realised I was causing you pain, I saw it in your eyes every time I looked at you. And when you started talking about babies and my leaving the army…' He rubbed his hand across his face. 'I couldn't do it. I knew you needed me but I believed the men needed me more. I had to choose.'

'You could have talked to me. Tried to explain. I loved you, Nick. I wouldn't have put you under more pressure.'

'You have to understand, Tiggy, none of this was clear in my head at that time. It was only later—after I was injured the first time—that I began to make some kind of sense of it. Even to myself.

'That's when I came looking for you. It had been four years since we'd separated, but I had to see you.'

'When you saw me with the twins?'

'Yes. I wanted to explain, apologise, I guess, for marrying you, letting you love me…' He shook his head again. 'I don't know what I expected. All I knew was that I needed to see you.'

'But you changed your mind and left?'

'After I rang the doorbell and there was no reply, I began to doubt you were even still living here, in which case I was planning to phone Charlie for your address. I was about to do that when you arrived. You were laughing as you got out of the car. You looked so beautiful, you took my breath away.'

'Go on,' she said quietly.

'I was watching you, drinking in the sight of you and cursing myself for letting you go. You went around to the boot and took out a pushchair. Then you reached out and took a baby from the back seat. And another one from the other side.'

'The twins,' Tiggy said.

'Yes. Melody and Chrissie. I know that now. But that day I thought they were yours. I thought you had found everything you'd ever wanted. Everything you deserved.' He rubbed a hand across his eyes.

'You looked so happy. I knew then I'd been hoping that somehow, despite everything, you'd be waiting for me.'

'I shouldn't have left. I should have tried harder to get you to talk to me. But when you told me you'd signed up for another tour, I thought…' Her voice hitched. 'I thought you'd fallen out of love with me. How could I have believed otherwise?'

'I never fell out of love with you. But, yes, when you

left, it was almost a relief. It meant I could return to Afghanistan without feeling guilty.'

Tiggy uncurled herself and crossed over to him. She sat on his lap and when he made to pull away from her she wrapped her arms around his neck. 'I don't want to talk any more. I don't want to think about the past—or the future.' She tugged his head down towards hers. 'I think it's time you kissed me.'

If sex had been good between them before, this time it was mind-blowing. It was if all the pain and longing Tiggy had felt over the years was poured into their lovemaking. When they'd finished they lay in each other's arms, not talking. What more was there to say? But for the first time since Nick had left, Tiggy felt whole again.

After a while they made love once more, slowly this time, savouring one another. Tiggy kissed every scar, memorising the feel of his body that was at once familiar but at the same time so very different. She wasn't going to think about the past or the future. All she wanted right at this moment was to be exactly where she was.

The next morning Tiggy lay in bed, listening to the clatter of Nick in the kitchen. He was whistling a tune she didn't recognise but he sounded happy.

As was she. It didn't matter that there was still so much that was unresolved between them. She now knew in her heart that Nick had never stopped loving her. The future was uncertain; she wasn't even sure that they could find a way back together, and she'd be risking her heart all over again, but it was too late. She loved him, and he loved her. Surely that was the most important thing? And this time they would talk. There would be no more secrets.

Nick came into the room, carrying a tray. She smiled

slowly when she saw that he was naked apart from the towel wrapped around his waist. She sat up, letting the sheet fall from her body. He placed the tray on the bedside table and grinned slowly. 'I guess coffee can wait, huh?'

The next few days were among the happiest Tiggy had known. They spent most of the time in bed, rediscovering each other's bodies. Neither of them talked about the future.

When they weren't in bed, they went for short runs together. This time it was Tiggy who ran backwards, teasing Nick about his inability to keep up. However, every day he was getting stronger. His limp had all but disappeared and his body was once more hard and muscled. In the evenings they took turns cooking and she showed Nick how to make omelettes and other simple dishes. Afterwards they would feed each other, prolonging the moment until they fell, laughing, into bed.

But of course it couldn't continue. This morning, the third time this week, she leaned over the sink hanging onto the edge for dear life before she was sick again. She could no longer even try to put it down to food poisoning. But that didn't mean she was pregnant.

She'd only had unprotected sex with Nick once, the first time, and since then they'd been careful to use contraception. Surely she couldn't have fallen pregnant?

Now, where had she heard that sort of denial before? Once was all it took. But her period could simply be late—stress and worry could do that, couldn't it?

She rinsed her face with cold water and sighed. Who was she trying to kid? Late periods were a pretty good indicator on their own, but put together with morning sickness...well, she'd have to have lost every ounce of common sense to deny the obvious. She was probably pregnant.

Pregnant. A tiny little baby was growing inside her. After thinking that motherhood might never be on the cards for her.

Nick's baby.

Nick, a father, whether he wanted to be or not.

Or not. Who was she kidding? Nick hadn't wanted to be a father six years ago. He had walked away from her then and she didn't know for sure that he'd wouldn't be walking away from her again. As soon as he was fit enough to pass his medical.

And although she loved him, although she would have given everything to have him around to be the father of her child, she wouldn't—couldn't—bear him to stay for the wrong reasons.

Which he would.

Tiggy washed her face and picked up her toothbrush. She almost didn't recognise the wild woman with burning eyes in the mirror. She smiled. Only a few weeks ago her life had been settled, a little bit boring perhaps but peaceful. Now she was reminded of those heady days in Afghanistan when she'd never felt more alive, and however Nick felt about being a father wouldn't change anything. She was going to have this baby.

But if she told him, would he feel trapped? Would he stay out of some misplaced sense of duty, something Nick did so well?

It wasn't as if she couldn't cope without him. Mum would help and her job paid well enough.

But she was getting ahead of herself. First things first. She had to know for sure if she was pregnant.

Then she would decide what, or if, to tell Nick.

CHAPTER SEVENTEEN

FINALLY IT WAS time for Nick to return to the hospital for an appointment with the physio, followed by a check-up with the medical team. If they were happy with his progress he would go through a full army medical in a couple of weeks' time and a decision would be made on whether or not he was fit to remain in the army—and if he could continue in emergency medicine.

Tiggy had no doubt what the answer would be, but she refused to think about what would happen after that. Having had a week off, it was time for her to go back to work. Nick had insisted that he didn't need her to come with him to the hospital.

It was late afternoon and she'd just returned home after her early shift when the doorbell rang. At first Tiggy assumed that it was Nick, but when she opened the door it was to find a young, attractive woman she didn't recognise standing on the doorstep.

'Can I help?' she asked. Perhaps she was looking for directions?

The woman bit her lip.

'Does a Nick Casey still live here?' she asked.

Tiggy froze. All at once all the old insecurities returned. God in heaven, was this one of Nick's girlfriends? If so, she was so young—at least half his age. A chill crept up her spine, to be replaced with an anger she hadn't known she was even capable of feeling.

'No,' Tiggy replied abruptly. 'Not for some time anyway.'

The rain was falling in a relentless sheet, soaking the woman. She didn't even seem to have an umbrella with her. Whoever she was, Tiggy couldn't leave her on the step. Besides, whatever the woman wanted with Nick, she had to know.

'Why don't you come in?'

'I don't want to disturb you.' The accent was American.

'Come in for a moment. At least to get dry.'

The woman hesitated for a few moments longer. Then she smiled. Instantly it lit up her face. She really was quite beautiful. 'If you're sure I'm not disturbing you?'

When her surprise guest was seated, Tiggy sat down opposite her. She decided to get straight to the point. 'How do you know Nick?'

'I don't really know him at all.'

'Oh?'

'He's my father.'

Tiggy was stunned. Whatever she'd expected, it hadn't been this. Nick had a daughter! A grown-up daughter. Why had he never said? Thoughts tumbled around her head. How could he have kept this from her?

'Nick is your father?' she said stupidly.

'Yes. At least, I think he is.' The girl took a photograph from her handbag and passed it to Tiggy. 'Is this him?'

It was definitely Nick. A much younger Nick but him nevertheless. She would have recognised those brown eyes and wide grin anywhere.

He wasn't alone in the photo. Next to him was a girl with brown hair and shining eyes, who was staring up at him lovingly.

'The woman?' Tiggy asked, her throat as dry as dust.
'My mother.'

Tiggy jumped to her feet. 'I'll just make some tea, shall I?' She needed a few moments alone to gather her thoughts. Nick had been seriously involved with someone before her, someone who had clearly adored him and with whom he'd had a child. How could he not have told her? What else had he kept from her? Was the woman in the photo, this girl, the real reason he'd left her six years ago? Had everything he'd told her been lies? She felt sick.

When she was satisfied she had her emotions under control, she returned to the sitting room. The girl leaped from the chair. 'I'm sorry. I haven't even told you my name. I'm Kate.'

'Hello, Kate. I'm Tiggy. Perhaps you should start from the beginning.'

For a second tears shimmered in Kate's eyes. Then she took a shuddering breath.

'I never knew my father. Mom would never talk about him. She died a month ago.'

Instinctively, Tiggy reached for her hand. 'I'm so sorry.'

'When I was going through her things I found that photo. I knew it had to be important to Mom. I asked around, but no one seemed to know who he was. All I could find out was that Mom had met a Brit when he was over on holiday, and by the time he'd left, she was pregnant.'

Nick was already a father. She couldn't get her head around what Kate was telling her.

'And now to get all the way here—to track him down to this address, only to find he's not here... I'll have to start looking for him all over again.'

Of course, Kate wouldn't have a clue that Nick had been in hospital.

Tiggy smiled grimly. Nick was going to get quite a shock. For whatever reason he'd kept his daughter a secret, there was no doubt he was going to come face to face with her.

'Your father is at the hospital. He's okay,' she added quickly, seeing the alarm in Kate's eyes. 'I mean, he's sort of okay. Look, I'd better tell you the whole story.'

By the time Tiggy had finished explaining it was almost dark.

'I need to see him,' Kate said.

'I'm bringing him back here tomorrow,' Tiggy said. 'Perhaps you should wait until then?'

But Kate was already gathering her bag, a determined look on her face. 'I've waited a long time to meet him. I don't want to wait any longer.'

'In that case, of course, I'll take you there.'

Tiggy left Kate at the hospital and sat in her car, watching the rain pour down the windscreen.

She was still reeling. Nick had a daughter and he was about to have another child. She couldn't begin to imagine how the news would affect a man who didn't want children.

She had been planning to tell him about the baby tonight, but now it would have to wait.

So she wouldn't tell him. At least not yet. Not until she had to.

CHAPTER EIGHTEEN

WHEN THE DOORBELL rang, Tiggy opened the door to find Nick standing there. He looked as if he had been caught up in an earthquake.

The rain was still falling steadily, his hair was plastered to his head and his eyes were wild.

'Why haven't you been answering my phone calls?' he said, stepping into the hall. 'I was worried about you.'

She stood aside to let him pass. 'Come in. You don't have to worry about me—ever. And I'm sure the internet has a list of good hotels.'

'I thought I was staying here?' he said, shocked.

'I've decided that's not a good idea.'

Puzzled, he took her by the shoulders. 'What is it, Tiggy?'

'You didn't think you should have told me you had a daughter?'

'So that's why you haven't being taking my calls.' He shook the rain from his hair like a dog who'd been for a swim. 'Kate told me she'd been to see you. I realise it must have been a shock but I thought she'd explained...'

'Explained what, exactly?'

'Let's sit down and talk,' Nick said firmly, taking her by the hand and leading her into the sitting room.

'I'm all ears, Nick,' Tiggy said grimly. 'But, believe me,

this is going to take some explaining. You have a child and you didn't think I should know?'

'I didn't know myself.' Nick looked at her in astonishment. Could it be he'd really had no idea he was a father? 'You don't think I would have kept that from you? You don't think I would have had a daughter and deliberately excluded her from my life?'

'How would I know? You kept everything else from me.' She wasn't going to let him off the hook that easily. It was as if all the trust she'd being allowing herself to feel over the last week or so had been washed away like a pile of sticks in a flood.

'I swear to you I had no idea,' Nick said, sitting down next to her. He cupped her face in his hands and forced her to look at him. 'Her mother never told me she was pregnant. It was a brief fling—I was only eighteen.'

Could she believe him? She desperately wanted to. But he'd kept so much from her.

'So what are you going to do now?'

'I don't know.' Suddenly he smiled. 'She's quite a girl. I think I'm going to enjoy having her around. If I can persuade her to stay for a while, that is.' He reached out for her. 'I missed you.'

She pulled away. 'I'm sorry, Nick. I don't know what we've been doing these last weeks but it can't last. Too much has happened. We can't turn the clocks back and pretend that we don't have a past.'

'Forget the past. Isn't it time we started talking about the future? The doctors gave me the all-clear. As far as they're concerned I'm fit for work. Now everything's back to normal, we can start thinking about having a life together again.'

She turned away from him. 'I don't think that's possible. I don't think I can ever trust you again. I'll always be wondering what you're not telling me.'

'Then let's not think about the future. Let's take it one day at a time.'

'I can't. I'm sorry, Nick. I just can't.'

He looked at her for one slow moment. 'I'm not going to let you give up on me, Tiggy, and I'm sure as hell not going to give up on you. We've been apart for too long.'

She stumbled to her feet. 'You're fine now, Nick. I think it's time you left.'

'Left?'

'Yes. Go back to the hotel. Go to Kate. Do whatever the hell you want to, but stay out of my life.'

Nick paced up and down the hotel room. He'd made a mess of it. But, then, had he really expected that it would be easy to win Tiggy back? She was right. If he was going to convince her that they were meant to be together, he needed to convince her first that he'd changed.

But how the hell was he going to do that? A few weeks ago he'd had no one outside his work expecting anything from him. Now he had two women, both of whom were a handful. Kate he could do nothing about, except be there for her in a way he hadn't been able to when she'd been a child, a fact that burned him up, and wait for her to learn she could rely on him. But Tiggy? How could he put that right?

Then it came to him. Their marriage had broken down because he'd been unable to share his life with her, because he'd treated her as someone who'd needed to be protected. He'd thought he'd been doing the best for her, but hadn't she made it clear to him that that was the very thing she couldn't bear?

She wasn't the woman he'd married—she was so much

more than that. She was strong, feisty and independent, and he loved her. And whatever she said, she loved him. But would she continue to love him when she knew everything there was to know about him?

There was only one way to find out. He picked up his mobile. It was time to call in a few favours.

Not for the first time Tiggy wondered if she was crazy. Nick had turned up at her door and insisted that she pack for a night away. When she'd tried to protest, he'd threatened to pack for her and to throw her in the back of the car along with her belongings.

'I've checked with the ward,' he said. 'You're not due on duty for a couple of days. I promise to have you back in plenty of time for your shift. Now, let me have your passport.'

Bewildered, Tiggy did as she was asked.

'Where are we going?' she asked as they headed north.

'I want to show you the place I spent my childhood.'

Tiggy was astounded. When they'd been married, she'd suggested several times that they visit Nick's old home in Ireland. But Nick had always refused, saying there was nothing in Ireland he cared to revisit. Eventually she'd stopped asking.

They took a flight to Dublin, where Nick had arranged for a hire car and from there they headed south.

'You should have asked Kate if she wanted to come,' Tiggy said. 'I'm sure she would have been interested.'

'Kate can come another time,' Nick said. 'Besides, she has plans for the next couple of days.'

The grim line of his mouth told Tiggy he wasn't pleased about something.

'You two haven't had a disagreement?'

'No, not exactly. It's just…'

'Just…?' Tiggy prompted.

'Oh, hell. It's Luke. My so-called doctor. I can't help but notice the way he's been looking at Kate. And I'd guess by the way she's behaving around him, she's not immune either.'

Tiggy hid a smile. Who would have thought? Nick acting the part of the concerned father. Except, judging by his expression, this was no act.

'So what's the problem? Luke's lovely, and Kate is clearly well able to take care of herself. She's not that much younger than I was when you went after me.'

'That was different,' Nick growled.

'And how exactly was it different?'

'Luke can't be taken seriously. I know stuff about his past I wish I didn't know—stuff that makes him a bad choice for Kate. And if that wasn't bad enough, he's a womaniser. You only have to see the way the nurses behave around him to know he has a reputation.'

This time Tiggy did laugh. 'And you were a saint when I met you? Do I need to tell you that I was warned off you the same way you want to warn off Kate? Trust me, Nick, don't even attempt it. Kate strikes me as a woman who can take care of herself. Just as I was,' she added softly.

'Sue was right, though, wasn't she? Perhaps you would have been better off if we'd never met.'

'Let's not go down that road again, Nick.' She gazed out of the window at the lush rolling hills. 'I wouldn't change a second of the time we had together, not even if it meant not having the pain.'

Nick didn't reply but his hands tightened on the steering wheel.

Some time later Nick stopped the car at the top of a field just past a small village. The sun was sinking in the sky but at this time of year there were a couple of hours yet before it got dark.

'You lived in a field?' Tiggy asked with a smile. Without waiting for him to reply, she opened the door and stepped out of the car. The air was like liquid oxygen after London and she breathed deeply. In the distance smoke curled from a farmhouse chimney and in the fields nearby a flock of sheep grazed contentedly.

'That was where I was brought up.' Nick pointed to the farmhouse.

'But it's beautiful!' she said honestly. 'How can anyone not love it here?'

Nick shook his head. 'You see what you want to see : an idyllic-looking farmhouse that you imagine is filled with love and laughter. It wasn't like that for me.' He took her by the hand. 'Come with me.'

She let him lead her down a narrow track. 'We owned the farmhouse. When my father died, Mum and I tried to carry on. I was eight. It didn't matter at first that I couldn't really help as there were others to do the outside work—farmworkers my father employed. We could have managed—if my mother hadn't fallen to pieces.'

He stopped by a flat rock and without saying anything they sat down.

'What happened?' Tiggy asked.

'She started drinking. She became depressed. To be honest, I don't know which came first. All I know is that the mother I loved turned into someone I didn't recognise. I would come home from school to find that she hadn't shopped, let alone cooked. It was obvious that she'd spent most of the day in bed. I got to know the smell of mints pretty well.'

Tiggy closed her eyes. She could see Nick as a boy.

Worse, she could feel that child's anger, bewilderment and hurt.

'I tried to look after her and the farm. Eventually the men who helped on the farm drifted away. I suspect Mum stopped paying them. One or two of their wives came to try and talk some sense into her but it was no use. I kept on trying. I cleaned and cooked as best I could—if you call tins of beans and bowls of cereal cooking. I milked the cows, cleaned out the barns, but it was no use. There was too much for a boy to do. I knew there wouldn't be enough hay to feed the cows in the winter but I also knew there was no money to buy any.

'I tried to speak to Mum. I begged her to get help. I pleaded, I shouted, I told her Dad would be ashamed to see the farm in such a state, but nothing got through to her.'

'Didn't the school try to help?'

'They tried to talk to me. I was falling behind with my schoolwork and falling asleep at my desk. But I wouldn't tell them about Mum. I was scared they would take me away. I kept on hoping that one day she would get up and be the mother she'd been before.'

He stared off into the distance and Tiggy reached for his hand.

'In the end we had to sell all the livestock. But still we struggled on. Until finally the bank foreclosed. We had to sell. And at a knock-down price. I persuaded Mum to keep the barn—that building over there.' He pointed to a ramshackle building about a hundred metres from the farmhouse. 'There was just about enough left over from the sale to make it habitable.'

Tiggy blinked. The building he was pointing to was tiny. Surely it wasn't big enough for two people to live in it?

'I fixed it up as best I could and we managed. Some-how. Then, when I was sixteen, Mum died.'

He swallowed.

'Oh, Nick. Why didn't you tell me any of this?'

'Because I was ashamed. I couldn't save the farm and I couldn't save my mother. I began to wonder if there was anything I *could* do.'

'You were a child!'

'I didn't feel like a child. I felt I had let them down. Mum and Dad. Dad would have expected me to look after Mum.'

'What did you do then?' Tiggy asked.

'I could have gone into care, but I didn't want that and as I was sixteen they couldn't make me. I made up my mind I would be a doctor. Perhaps then I could do some good. My grades in school were rubbish but I had two years left to sit exams that would get me into university. When I wasn't at school I spent every spare minute at the library.'

He smiled. 'At least it was warm there. I managed to get a job at the local hospital as a night porter when I was seventeen, although I made myself a year older on my application. At nights when I wasn't working I was in the hospital library, learning anything and everything I could find in medical textbooks. One advantage: I learned to do without sleep. I passed my exams—all A stars—and applied to medical school. Edinburgh accepted me.

'It was still impossible financially so I joined the army as a cadet as a way of funding myself through medical school. Turned out it was the best decision of my life. I loved the army. After my chaotic upbringing I liked the order: the way meals were at certain times; the way there was a time and a place for everything. And years of working on the farm had left me strong and so I thrived on the physical challenges of being in the army.' He turned to look at her. 'I knew I had come home.'

* * *

It explained so much, but why hadn't he told her this before? She would never have given up on him had she known.

'Would you like to see the barn?' he asked.

'Won't the owners object?'

'I checked. They're away for a few days but they said to help myself. They use the barn as a self-catering rental during the summer.'

They walked hand in hand down the track until they came to the door of the house. Nick bent and retrieved the key from under a stone. He grinned and suddenly the sadness left his eyes. 'Exactly where I used to leave it.'

He unlocked the door and stepped aside to allow Tiggy to go in before him. The little house was dark, the only light coming from two small windows, and it took her eyes a few moments to adjust. There was an open fireplace in one thick wall with a couple of chairs in front of it, a small kitchen to the side and a double bed against the other wall, taking up most of the remainder of the space. Cosy for a weekend retreat, but for two people to live?

'There was a sofa where the chairs are now,' Nick said. 'It doubled up as my bed. Until Mum died. '

He glanced around the room. 'Mum had her bed where this one is now and I put up a curtain for her so she could have some privacy. As it was only a single, it left some space for my desk.'

He pointed to the fireplace. 'Mum did have her good days, especially in the beginning. Sometimes we used to toast marshmallows over the fire and she would tell me about her childhood. She came from Belfast. Sadly her parents wanted nothing to do with her when she married a man from the south.' He rubbed his hand across his forehead. 'I think that's enough reminiscing for a moment.

How do you feel about staying here tonight? I could light a fire.'

'Can you bear to stay here with all its memories?'

He breathed deeply. 'You know, Tiggy, I'm glad I came. All my life I've been dreaming of this house, and those dreams haven't been pleasant. But it doesn't look anything like it used to.'

Tiggy couldn't bear it any longer. She crossed over to Nick and wound her arms around his neck.

'Come, my darling,' she said. 'I think we should lay these ghosts to rest for once and for all.'

Later, when they'd had their fill of one another and were lying in each other's arms, Tiggy looked up at Nick. Whatever she tried to tell herself, she knew she was where she needed to be.

The morning sun and the smell of frying bacon woke Tiggy to a new day.

Nick, wearing only a pair of jeans, was at the cooker, fighting with the bacon, which appeared ready to go up in smoke. Tiggy leaped from the bed, rescued the bacon and retrieved the toast, which was threatening to go the same way. 'You know, for a man with a hero's reputation you're pretty useless in the kitchen. I'm surprised you didn't starve as a boy!'

Nick stood back. 'Give me complicated surgery any time.'

After breakfast they tidied the house and left the key under the stone. On their way back to the airport, Nick pulled up alongside a church on the outskirts of a village.

'This is where I was christened,' he said. 'And where my parents are buried.'

'Shall we see if we can find their graves?' Tiggy asked.

'I know exactly where they are.'

He led her through the gate and to the side of the church, before coming to stop in front of a simple stone engraved with the names and dates of Eleanor and Jack Casey.

'I couldn't afford a separate stone for my mother at the time,' Nick said softly.

Tiggy reached for his hand and squeezed it. 'You did everything you could for her. It wasn't within your power to save her.'

'I know. At least, I know that now.'

'Shall we go inside?'

Nick shrugged. 'If you like. There's not much to see.'

The church was small but had the most exquisite stained-glass windows. It was more beautiful to Tiggy than any cathedral. She sat in the front pew and let the peace wash over her.

Nick sat next to her. 'Maybe one day we can renew our vows here? Start over again?'

She imagined Nick as a baby, being christened at the altar, being brought up on the farm as happy as a pig in clover, then his life going so badly wrong. She could understand him now. She could even understand why their marriage hadn't survived. But a little piece of her still wondered if it was too late for them.

'With a baby?' she asked tentatively. 'In time?'

Nick took her by the hands. 'I'm not sure I can be the kind of father I want to be, and I still need to get my head around the fact I already have a daughter.' He folded his fingers around hers. 'But if it's what you want...'

His reply wasn't good enough. She needed him to want this baby as much as she did.

'Let's wait and see, Nick.'

CHAPTER NINETEEN

A FEW DAYS after they returned to London, Tiggy received a phone call from Alice.

'Please, can you take them for the night?' she begged as soon as pleasantries were over. 'Charlie's on long haul and my mother's feeling poorly. I would take the twins with me but you know what a handful they can be. Your mother has something on she can't get out of and your dad finds it difficult to cope with them on his own. I wouldn't ask if I wasn't desperate. I know you have a lot on your plate, what with Nick and everything.' She dropped her voice. 'How's that going, by the way?'

'Of course I'll take the twins,' Tiggy reassured her, ignoring the question. The truth was she didn't know how she and Nick were doing. Since they'd returned from Ireland they'd resumed their earlier routine without returning to the topic of the future. 'I haven't seen Chrissie and Melody for ages. I've missed them.'

'You've probably forgotten what a handful they can be,' Alice replied dryly. 'But thanks, Tiggy. I owe you.'

They arranged that Alice would drop the girls off on her way to her mother's in an hour.

Nick wandered into the kitchen to wash his hands. He'd bought an old Harley-Davidson and was restoring it. He'd go mad, he'd said, if he didn't have something to do. Although he'd passed his medical, he was still on leave until he'd been assessed by the army doctors. He looked so sexy in his T-shirt with the sleeves cut off, his faded jeans and a smear of grease up one arm.

'You don't fancy holding the tools for me while I work?' he asked.

'Sorry. No can do. Twin invasion on the horizon.'

'Perhaps they could hold the tools?'

Tiggy laughed. 'Nick, they're four years old!'

Nick wrapped his arms around her waist and nuzzled her neck. 'Do we have time to slip upstairs before they arrive?'

'We most certainly do not.' But when Nick continued trailing kisses down her neck, her knees went weak. 'Perhaps if we're quick?'

They only just managed to shower and dress before the twins arrived. The little girls ran into the house like two miniature tornadoes. 'Aunty Tiggy! Uncle Nick! We want to go to Hamleys. Mummy says if we ask nicely you might take us. Please say yes!'

Tiggy sighed. A visit to the toy superstore wasn't her first choice of a day out. But when the girls looked at Nick with their butter-wouldn't-melt-in-my-mouth expressions, he immediately agreed.

'What is Hamleys anyway?' he asked Tiggy as the girls did a victory dance around the kitchen.

'Looks like you're about to find out.'

Nick looked through the kitchen window, towards his bike, which was waiting in the driveway. A tortured look crossed his face. 'I guess the bike can wait. Lead me to this place—whatever it is.'

'It's a toy store!' Nick said, sounding aghast as Tiggy hurried inside after the excited twins. He whistled under his breath. 'Good God, it's the size of a multi-storey car park.'

Melody and Chrissie were tugging at Tiggy's arms. 'Come on, Aunty Tiggy,' Melody pleaded. 'I want to see the doll's house.'

Chrissie's mouth settled into a line that didn't bode well. '*I* want to see the fairy-tale stuff.'

Tiggy turned to a still shell-shocked-looking Nick. 'I don't suppose...'

Nick sent her the ghost of a smile. 'I'll take one, you take the other.' He picked Chrissie up and tossed her into the air. She sent him a look that would have cowed lesser men. 'Please, put me down, Uncle Nick. I'm not a baby.'

'Okay.' Nick placed her back on the ground and raised his eyebrows at Tiggy, who suppressed a smile. She had no idea how he was going to cope with a couple of hours of Chrissie but she was looking forward to finding out.

After she and Melody had visited almost every department in the store and they still hadn't come across Nick and Chrissie, Tiggy was beginning to worry. But to her relief she spotted them eventually in the toy train department. Nick was sitting cross-legged with Chrissie on his lap as they watched the trains going around.

'So here you are,' Tiggy said.

Chrissie and Nick glanced at her before turning their attention back to the train set. 'Finished already?' Nick asked over his shoulder.

'It's been more than two hours, Nick. Aren't you and Chrissie hungry?'

Nick glanced at his watch. 'Two hours! No way. Anyway...' he ruffled Chrissie's curls, almost exactly the way he'd used to ruffle Tiggy's '...we've had a snack.'

When Chrissie did turn round Tiggy could see that they had indeed. Chrissie's mouth was covered in chocolate.

'We had chocolate milkshake *and* chocolate cake,' she said.

''S not fair,' Melody complained. 'Aunty Tiggy made me have yucky soup. She said I needed something proper for lunch.'

Nick removed Chrissie from his lap and stood up. 'Sorry, Tigs,' he said, looking sheepish. 'Guess I don't make a very good babysitter.'

Chrissie looked up at him adoringly. 'You're the best babysitter ever,' she said staunchly. 'Now, can we go back to our trains?'

CHAPTER TWENTY

A COUPLE OF days later, when Nick returned from his army medical, he was grinning. Tiggy's heart sank. Although she was glad he'd passed, she couldn't bear to think he was going away again.

'You passed, then,' she said.

'Yes.'

'You'll be going back to Afghanistan?'

'Actually, I won't.' Nick looked at her. 'I've asked for a permanent post in the military hospital in Birmingham. Or, if you don't want to move, I'll resign from the army and look for a job in London.'

It was the last thing she'd expected.

'Why?' She needed him to spell it out.

'Because I don't want to leave you again. I want the life I had and thought I didn't want. I was wrong. I lost the woman I loved most in the world and I'm not going to lose her again.' He crouched by her chair. 'I've been such a fool, Tiggy. My life is nothing without you, never has been, never will be. I know it'll take time for you to learn to trust me again, but I can wait. I can, and will, wait forever.'

She closed her eyes. Could she believe him?

'I'm learning, Tigs. I'm learning that being a family means responsibility, but that it can be good too. Kate and I have a lot of lost time to make up, but we're making progress. I'd like you to meet her properly. I want the two most important women in my life to get to know each other.'

'Looks like you've taken to being a father.' If he could be a decent father to Kate, perhaps he could be one to their child too?

'It still feels weird, but I'm learning family life can be fun. The other day, when we were at Hamleys with the girls, I realised that there are many ways to be a parent. I might not always get it right, but that doesn't matter. If there's enough love, like there is between you and your family, like Charlie and Alice have with their children, it can be good. Great even. Responsibility doesn't always have to feel bad.'

Something inside her chest shifted. It was what she'd been longing to hear. 'Your parents would have been proud of you. You do know that, don't you?'

'I did my best. It was all I could do. And you're right, the soldiers on the front line have the best medical personnel in the country to look after them. I don't want to look back any more. Life's too short.'

He pulled her to her feet and placed his hands on either side of her face. 'I know I have no right to ask you. I know I've hurt you badly. I would understand if you couldn't forgive me, but if I can't have you, I won't have anyone.'

She turned her face up to his. There were no guarantees in life, but she believed him when he said he loved her.

'Shut up and kiss me,' she demanded.

Of course they ended up in bed together.

Nick's hands were cupping her hips, sweeping like feathers over her stomach sending ripples of liquid heat straight to her pelvis. Suddenly he paused and ran his hands over her abdomen again, before returning to her breasts. A look of wonder filled his eyes. 'Tiggy, are you pregnant?'

She gazed up at the man who, for better or for worse, she loved and would always love, no matter what pain he'd caused her, no matter if the future with him would always be like a roller-coaster. She would rather spend one minute in hell with him than a lifetime without him.

'Do you mind?'

He laughed and rolled over on his back, pulling her on top of him. 'Mind?' His hands caressed her bottom. 'It's perfect. You're perfect. Our whole bloody lives are going to be perfect.'

She smiled down at him. 'Maybe not perfect, at least not always, but pretty damn close.'

* * * * *

Mills & Boon® Hardback

September 2013

ROMANCE

Challenging Dante	Lynne Graham
Captivated by Her Innocence	Kim Lawrence
Lost to the Desert Warrior	Sarah Morgan
His Unexpected Legacy	Chantelle Shaw
Never Say No to a Caffarelli	Melanie Milburne
His Ring Is Not Enough	Maisey Yates
A Reputation to Uphold	Victoria Parker
A Whisper of Disgrace	Sharon Kendrick
If You Can't Stand the Heat...	Joss Wood
Maid of Dishonour	Heidi Rice
Bound by a Baby	Kate Hardy
In the Line of Duty	Ami Weaver
Patchwork Family in the Outback	Soraya Lane
Stranded with the Tycoon	Sophie Pembroke
The Rebound Guy	Fiona Harper
Greek for Beginners	Jackie Braun
A Child to Heal Their Hearts	Dianne Drake
Sheltered by Her Top-Notch Boss	Joanna Neil

MEDICAL

The Wife He Never Forgot	Anne Fraser
The Lone Wolf's Craving	Tina Beckett
Re-awakening His Shy Nurse	Annie Claydon
Safe in His Hands	Amy Ruttan

0813 GEN STD HB

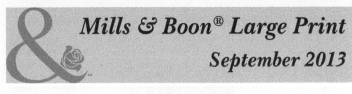

Mills & Boon® Large Print

September 2013

ROMANCE

A Rich Man's Whim	Lynne Graham
A Price Worth Paying?	Trish Morey
A Touch of Notoriety	Carole Mortimer
The Secret Casella Baby	Cathy Williams
Maid for Montero	Kim Lawrence
Captive in his Castle	Chantelle Shaw
Heir to a Dark Inheritance	Maisey Yates
Anything but Vanilla...	Liz Fielding
A Father for Her Triplets	Susan Meier
Second Chance with the Rebel	Cara Colter
First Comes Baby...	Michelle Douglas

HISTORICAL

The Greatest of Sins	Christine Merrill
Tarnished Amongst the Ton	Louise Allen
The Beauty Within	Marguerite Kaye
The Devil Claims a Wife	Helen Dickson
The Scarred Earl	Elizabeth Beacon

MEDICAL

NYC Angels: Redeeming The Playboy	Carol Marinelli
NYC Angels: Heiress's Baby Scandal	Janice Lynn
St Piran's: The Wedding!	Alison Roberts
Sydney Harbour Hospital: Evie's Bombshell	Amy Andrews
The Prince Who Charmed Her	Fiona McArthur
His Hidden American Beauty	Connie Cox

0813 GEN STD LP

Mills & Boon® Hardback
October 2013

ROMANCE

The Greek's Marriage Bargain	Sharon Kendrick
An Enticing Debt to Pay	Annie West
The Playboy of Puerto Banús	Carol Marinelli
Marriage Made of Secrets	Maya Blake
Never Underestimate a Caffarelli	Melanie Milburne
The Divorce Party	Jennifer Hayward
A Hint of Scandal	Tara Pammi
A Façade to Shatter	Lynn Raye Harris
Whose Bed Is It Anyway?	Natalie Anderson
Last Groom Standing	Kimberly Lang
Single Dad's Christmas Miracle	Susan Meier
Snowbound with the Soldier	Jennifer Faye
The Redemption of Rico D'Angelo	Michelle Douglas
The Christmas Baby Surprise	Shirley Jump
Backstage with Her Ex	Louisa George
Blame It on the Champagne	Nina Harrington
Christmas Magic in Heatherdale	Abigail Gordon
The Motherhood Mix-Up	Jennifer Taylor

MEDICAL

Gold Coast Angels: A Doctor's Redemption	Marion Lennox
Gold Coast Angels: Two Tiny Heartbeats	Fiona McArthur
The Secret Between Them	Lucy Clark
Craving Her Rough Diamond Doc	Amalie Berlin

0913 GEN STD HB

Mills & Boon® Large Print

October 2013

ROMANCE

HISTORICAL

MEDICAL

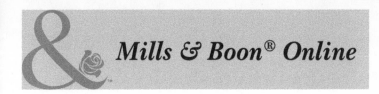